THE INN ON HARMONY ISLAND

SWEET TEA AND A SOUTHERN GENTLEMAN
BOOK 1

ANNE-MARIE MEYER

"We're all a little broken somehow. All we can hope to find in this life is that person who gathers and protects all of our broken pieces until we're ready to heal."

MILES

USA TODAY BESTSELLING AUTHOR

ANNE-MARIE
MEYER

THE INN ON
HARMONY
ISLAND

SWEET TEA &
SOUTHERN GENTLEMAN
1

For Every Person who has Felt Broken
There are People Collecting your Broken Pieces

PROLOGUE

Shelby

I'D NEVER NOTICED the way rain looked as it fell into puddles. The tiny splashes each drop made caused smaller drops to spray around it. The ripples would go for only a moment until another drop would fall, and the effect would happen all over again.

A low murmur of *amens* drew my focus away from the puddles. I wrapped my black shawl tighter around my shoulders as I turned to the pastor who was standing behind my grandmother's coffin. He was speaking, but in all honesty, I couldn't hear what he was saying. My stomach was a bundle of nerves since I drove the rental car into my small hometown, and I couldn't sort out anyone's words.

I'd left this place 10 years ago, never to return. That

was, until Gran up and passed away. I couldn't very well *not* go to her funeral. So, I packed my carry-on and flew down from New York to face the past that I'd tried so hard to forget.

And here I was, staring my history straight in the face.

I sighed as I ducked my head down. Miles's body tightened next to me when our arms brushed. I glanced over at him to see his jaw muscles flex, but his gaze never wavered from the pastor's face.

Was it strange that my ex-stepbrother was more broken up about my grandmother's passing than me?

I pursed my lips and turned my attention to my lap.

Yes, that was strange. And sad. And pathetic.

Even though I wanted to console my ego and convince myself that it was okay that Miles had cried more times than I had during the funeral planning. That the funeral director handed *him* the box of tissues and never offered them to me. Nothing I could say to myself would fix the cold, hard heart my past had left me with.

I wanted to cry. I really did. But it was as if my tears were dried up. There was nothing left. I'd cried so much in the past that it was as if my body was completely incapable of producing tears. I was broken, and this was proof that I was never going to be fixed.

My body turned numb as I watched the cemetery owner lower the coffin into the ground. Even though it was raining, the early spring heat surrounded us. Mr. Jorgenson, the town's mayor, wiped his forehead with his handkerchief before stuffing it back into his suit coat. Most of the other guests were leaving, sprinting to their cars with their hands or purses over their heads. The women were slowed by their heels digging into the soft ground.

I glanced down at the dark oak coffin in the ground, wondering for a moment if Gran would have been disappointed with what we'd chosen. Even though it had been years since we'd spoken, I still wanted to please her. To settle her into her final resting place in comfort.

Movement next to me drew my attention over. Miles was standing a few yards off, shaking hands with the pastor who then nodded and turned to hurry through the rain to his car.

We were now officially alone.

Miles hesitated; his gaze focused on something in front of him. But then, as if he could feel my gaze, he turned.

I knew I should look away. Facing Miles—facing Harmony Island—was the last thing I wanted to do. But I couldn't drop my gaze. The familiarity in his stormy blue eyes as they peered into my soul paralyzed me. Miles had been my protector when we were kids, but then our parents divorced and something in him changed in high school. Our relationship was never the same. Especially now, when he seemed closer to my grandmother than I could ever be. That stung as bad as the wasps from the nest we knocked down as kids.

I shivered and focused on the hole in front of me. I was done thinking about Miles. I was finished thinking about our past. But as soon as I saw Miles approach me from the corner of my eye, I sucked in my breath.

I cursed myself. Why had I allowed our gazes to meet? I'd spent most of my three days here giving short answers and keeping to myself in the only motel in town. The other lodging options, Harmony Island Inn and the Apple Blossom B&B, were places I swore I would never go.

Too many bad memories roamed the halls.

"You okay?" Miles's voice was low and rumbly. I wasn't sure if it was because of our history or the situation we were in.

I nodded, tightening my grip on my upper arms. "I'm just glad it's over. I'm ready to get out of here." Miles remained quiet. I peeked over at him, worried that I'd said the wrong thing. "I mean—"

"I know what you mean." Miles slipped off his suit coat, folded it in half, and rested it on the chair behind him. Then he yanked at his tie and loosened the top two buttons of his white shirt. After ruffling his gelled hair, he began to unbutton his cuffs and roll up his sleeves. "She never wanted you to stay away, but she understood why you left."

His words were like poison to my soul. It was easier to believe that my grandmother hated me than to think she'd spent her life waiting for me to return. When I was in New York, I could pretend that we had a mutual under-standing. Our family was toxic. A broken mix of flawed people that fate stupidly threw together. My grandmother, my mother, and me.

We were the opposite of the three musketeers. We were a mixture of oil, water, and alcohol. Three pieces of a puzzle that would never fit together. Now, they were both gone. My senior year of high school, Mom ran away with her yoga instructor and died in a car crash.

With Gran in the ground, I was the only one alive.

I was the only one left carrying the burden of the failure that was our small, dysfunctional family.

"I doubt that," I whispered as I tucked a few strands of hair behind my ear that the cool ocean breeze had managed to free from the tight bun at the nape of my neck.

Miles finished rolling his sleeve and glanced over at me. I could see that he was fighting his response, and the truth was, I didn't want to hear it. It was easier when I didn't think anyone cared.

"So, are you leaving us for good then?"

His question caught me off guard. *Leaving us.* I hated that he'd moved into my life, my hometown, and my past like this. If I had my way, we would sell Harmony Island Inn and never look back.

"Yes," I responded, nodding my head.

"And the will? Are you going to come back for the reading?"

I took in a deep breath and tipped my head back, closing my eyes. "We both know that she didn't leave me anything."

"We do?"

I opened my eyes, looking up at the white canopy that protected us from the rain. "Despite what you say, she wrote me out of her life a long time ago. There's no point in pretending otherwise."

"Shelby—"

"Miles, I'm tired." I pulled my phone out of my purse and opened my rideshare app.

Miles stepped forward with his hand extended. For a moment, I caught what looked like desperation in his gaze before it disappeared. "Why don't I give you a ride? I mean, the church organized a dinner and everything." His half smile was weak and did little to dissuade me from what I'd already decided. "The town...misses you."

I snorted as I looked up at him. Then I shook my head and returned to filling out my information and sending in the request. "I seriously doubt that." I sighed. "I'm going to go back to my hotel room and jump in the shower. My flight is early in the morning, and I can't be late."

"Oh."

I hated that he seemed disappointed. But I needed him to move on. Returning to my one-bedroom apartment in New York where I could bury my memories until they were good and dead was the only thing holding me together.

"Listen, I know my grandmother meant a lot to you, but let's not pretend that there's anything left for me here.

Our family is finished." My voice cracked at the last word, which threw me off guard.

I hoped Miles didn't hear my last sentence, but after seeing the small quirk of his eyebrow, regret filled my chest.

He'd heard.

I cleared my throat. "Thank you for taking care of my grandmother in the last moments of her life." I brushed my hands down my black dress, desperate for something to do. The mixture of my grandmother's coffin in front of me and the way Miles was studying me, tugged at the fraying strands that were barely holding my life together.

But I knew if I didn't thank him, the pressure to acknowledge that he was the better grandchild would gnaw at me until I would eventually buy another plane ticket to come down here and confess it. I wanted this to be the last trip I made to my godforsaken hometown. I needed to make sure I tied up all my loose ends with a pretty little bow.

"Of course," Miles said. "She helped me a lot." His voice deepened as he turned to face the hole where my grandmother now lay. His shoulders slumped, and I suddenly felt sorry.

I felt sorry for him. I felt sorry for my grandmother. And I felt sorry for me.

No one had it perfect. We'd messed up so bad that, sometimes, the best thing to do was to call a foul and walk away.

And that was what I was determined to do.

My phone dinged, startling us both. I lifted it up so I could see the screen.

"My ride's here," I whispered.

Miles pushed his hands through his hair once more and nodded. "Yeah, okay." Then he paused.

I could see in his body language that he wanted to say something more, and I had a sinking suspicion as to what that was. Problem was, there was no way I was ready to hear any of it.

"It's been nice knowing you," I said. And before I could stop myself, I reached out and rested my hand on his arm. His warm skin shocked my fingertips, and I blinked and pulled my hand back, cursing myself for doing that.

What was wrong with me?

Miles's gaze dropped down to the spot I had touched before he brought his gaze up to meet mine. His dark blue eyes had turned stormy, which caused my stomach to flip-flop.

My phone chimed again, pulling me from my thoughts. I pushed my purse strap higher up onto my shoulder and then gave him a weak smile.

"Goodbye, Miles," I said as I stepped around him.

He didn't say anything as I passed by. It wasn't until I'd stepped out into the rain, raising my purse up over my head that I heard his response.

"Goodbye, Shelby."

Like a dam breaking inside of me, the tears began to

flow. I was grateful for the rain now more than ever. My tears mixed with the water running down my face as I crossed the cemetery lawn and pulled open the door of the black SUV.

The man asked for my name, and I managed to get that out. He didn't say much else as he put the car into drive and took off down the small, one-lane road that led to Main Street.

Thankfully, he didn't ask me what was wrong. Being picked up at a cemetery seemed to be all he needed to know. Hiding under that excuse, I allowed the tears that had refused to fall all of this time to flow. I was hurt. I was broken. And for this moment, I was going to allow myself to be weak.

As soon as I got back to New York, I'd forget. But for now, I didn't have the strength.

1

SHELBY

Six Months Later

THE KNOCK on my door startled me. I pulled my gaze away from my computer monitor and blinked a few times. My eyes were sore from staring at bouquet options, and it took a moment for them to readjust.

I cleared my throat as I pushed away from my desk and called out, "Come in."

The door burst open, and standing in the entryway was Sara, the new intern my boss had hired. Her hair was disheveled and her cheeks pink. She was huffing like she'd just run a marathon and was trying to catch her breath.

I quirked an eyebrow. "Everything okay?" I asked.

She doubled over, clutching her ribs and took a few big, deep breaths.

Concern filled my chest as I stood and moved to cross

the room. Before I reached her, she lifted her finger to stop me. "It's...okay..." she said between breaths. "Phone call... line one."

I glanced back to the phone on my desk where the "line 1" light was blinking, before bringing my attention back to her. Whoever was on the other line could wait. "But are you okay?" I asked, dipping down so I could catch her gaze.

Sara whipped up, surprising me enough to step back. Her whole face was bright red now from the blood that must have rushed to her head. She smiled and shrugged. "I got Patricia's coffee order wrong, and I had to race back to the coffee shop before she noticed." Sara's breathing had steadied, and her normally cheerful demeanor was back.

I nodded, contemplating for a moment if I should tell her that she was trying too hard to make our boss like her. But I pinched my lips shut. I'd just been promoted to assistant project manager, and there was no way I wanted to go back to a reception job. Not when I'd gotten this far.

The wedding industry was cutthroat, and if I wanted to own my own wedding planning business someday, I needed to keep climbing. Sara was sweet, but I knew if roles were reversed, she'd do the same with me.

"Well, keep hydrated," I said as I rested my hand on my lower back and pressed, stretching out the tension that had taken up residence there. We were in the middle of planning a wedding for some billionaire, and there'd been way too many late nights.

Sara nodded. "I will." Then she wiggled her finger in the direction of the phone. "Make sure you get that."

"Yes, ma'am." My southern drawl slipped out. My cheeks hinted pink as I pinched my lips together. I'd gone to great lengths to keep my background hidden. My past was dead. The last thing I needed was for anyone to know where I'd come from.

I was determined to reinvent myself here, and lugging my past around with me like a ball and chain wasn't going to help. To everyone here, I was Shelby Sorenson, *the* wedding planner to watch.

"Let me know if you need anything," she said.

I nodded as I rounded my desk and picked up the receiver. Not sure who it was, I waited until Sara left, shutting the door behind her, before I brought it to my ear.

"Hello?" a deep, soothing voice asked.

I paused and blinked. That sounded like Miles. Which was strange. I hadn't spoken to him or seen him since Gran's funeral. Why was he calling me now?

"Miles?"

Silence. "Shelby?"

I grabbed my chair's armrest and pulled it over so I could sit down. My back was straight as I sat there, waiting to hear why he'd purposely disobeyed my request to be left alone. "Yeah, you called me."

"Right. Sorry."

I sighed as I collapsed against the back of my chair. "What do you want?"

He cleared his throat. "Listen, I know you didn't want me to contact you."

"Yes," I said, probably a bit too quickly.

He paused. "But there's no way around this."

I hated how hesitant he sounded. I'd grown up with the kid. He was beating around the bush, and there was only one reason for that. He wanted to ask me to do something he knew I had no interest in doing.

"What do you need from me?" I bent the corner of my desktop calendar and then flattened it, pressing my nail along the crease.

"Tom said there's no way I can do this without you."

"Do what?" I furrowed my brow. "And who's Tom?"

Miles cleared his throat. "Tom's the lawyer that is helping me with Gran's will."

I swallowed, stress rising in my throat and forming a ball. "Will?"

"Yeah." He sighed. "You need to come back to Harmony Island."

I shook my head. "I'm not coming back. I told you at the funeral. I'm done."

"I know you said that, but..." His voice trailed off.

I glanced down at the receiver. Had we been cut off? "Miles?" I asked, praying that he was still on the line. The last thing I needed was to have to call him and go through this once more.

"Yeah, sorry."

"But what?" I was desperate for this conversation to end.

"If you don't come back, the state will seize the property."

I closed my eyes and took in a deep breath. There was a part of me that wanted to say, "Good, let them take that godforsaken place." But the other part of me, the part that could feel my grandmother's disappointment from the grave, screamed louder. I may hate the fact that I shared a past with that woman, but it didn't overshadow the fact that losing her inn to people who wouldn't respect it was the last thing she would want to happen.

Plus, I didn't want her haunting me from the grave.

"I promise if you come here, I'll stay out of your way." Miles's tone had turned deeper. "I heard Missy is looking to get funds to buy it as soon as it goes up for auction."

My heart stopped entirely. The room around me turned hazy. I could hear my heart pound in my ears.

Missy.

I hadn't heard that name in years. The last time someone uttered it in my presence was when I was stuffing my luggage into a taxi, the night I left Harmony Island for good.

She was the mother of the man who broke my heart ten years ago.

"Missy?" I squeaked out.

Miles was quiet. I knew he was quite aware of what

that name would do to me. He'd lived it with me. Miles was part of the reason I was such a wreck.

"Yes," he said quietly.

I pressed my fingers to my temple and kneaded the pressure that had built up there. I didn't want to go back. Who knew what my grandmother had put in her will. The last thing I wanted was to stay there longer than I needed.

Regardless, with all those fears coursing through my body, there was one specific fear that rose to the top. The one that had my head aching and my heart pounding. It was the fear that Clint Hodges's mother would buy the inn my family owned.

"How long will this take?" I whispered, keeping my eyes closed.

"Tom plans to read it on Monday."

"Monday?" At least I'd have the weekend to prep.

"Yeah."

I sighed as I slowly opened my eyes. "You'll stay out of my way?"

Silence. "If that's what you want."

Tears pricked my eyes. I hated that this was our relationship now. We'd been friends once. And then his actions drove the man I loved away from me. Now, Miles and I were just...nothing. I tried not to think about Miles, Clint, and Harmony Island. But no matter how hard I tried, I couldn't quite run far away enough from them.

"Fine," I whispered. "I'll be there for the reading."

He let out a relieved sigh. "Thank you."

I nodded but then felt stupid. He couldn't see me. "I'm just ready to get this over with," I said, swallowing hard on the emotions that had lodged themselves in my throat.

"I know," he said, his voice deepening. "I'll see you on Monday."

I didn't say goodbye; I just pressed the hang-up button and returned the phone to the base. Then I leaned back in my chair, tipped my face toward the ceiling, and closed my eyes.

So many emotions were rushing through me, a tear slipped down my cheek. I needed a moment to compose myself before I got back to work.

Beep

I startled and stared at my intercom. The notification came again. I quickly wiped the tear away and pulled my receiver off the base, cradling it between my cheek and shoulder. "Yeah?" I asked.

"Patricia needs you in her office," Sara said, this time, her cadence was calm. She must be sitting at her desk, waiting for the next errand Patricia would send her on.

"Right now?" I asked, wiping my cheeks once more. If Patricia saw my tear-stained face she'd ask what the issue was. The last thing I needed was for her to think I couldn't handle this job.

Especially since I needed to ask for some time off.

"Yep," she said, emphasizing the *p*.

"I'll be right there." I hung up the phone, grabbed my suit jacket, and slipped it on as I pushed through the door and out to the lobby. I tapped my toe on the hard marble floor as I waited for the elevator doors to open.

I boarded, grateful the elevator was empty. I crossed my arms and watched the numbers climb up slowly. When the car reached the tenth floor, it stopped and the doors slid open.

Michelle, Patricia's assistant, was sitting at her desk. The sound of fake fingernails typing on a keyboard filled the air. I gave her a quick nod and then pointed toward Patricia's closed door. "She wanted me?" I asked as I headed toward her office.

Michelle didn't look up as she nodded and reached over to her intercom. "Shelby's here to see you," she said before returning to her computer.

"Send her in," Patricia's voice came through the speaker.

I didn't wait for Michelle's instructions as I pushed the doors open and entered.

Patricia was sitting at her desk. Her inky black hair was pulled up into a severe ponytail. Her soft, ivory skin was taut, and her red lips contrasted against her appearance.

She flicked her gaze over at me before returning to her computer screen. "Have a seat," she said.

Something about the tone of her voice and the way she refused to look directly at me always threw me off. I felt like I was a little kid again, sitting outside of the principal's office, waiting to see if I was in trouble.

I hated that she didn't make me feel calm when that was all I needed right now.

"Yes, ma'am," I muttered, my southern drawl slipping again from my lips. My cheeks flushed as Patricia's gaze flicked at me. I prayed she hadn't heard and settled down on the chair across from her desk.

The sound of typing filled the air as Patricia finished her business. This wasn't uncommon for her. She would always invite you into her office but then make you wait.

You were left wondering what the meeting was going to be about. And sweating buckets while the worst possibilities flooded your mind.

I sat there with my hands on my thighs, tapping my fingers. I glanced around with the strange hope that there might be something on the walls, her bookshelves, or her desk that could tell me why I was here.

Thankfully, the clicking of her keyboard stopped, and she turned to face me before my entire body went numb from anxiety.

"Shelby."

"Y-yes?" I pinched my lips shut for a moment before I cleared my throat and repeated, "Yes."

Patricia studied me. Her expression was unreadable. "How long have you been with me?"

I shrugged. "Two—er, three years." Why was she asking this? I wasn't due for a job evaluation anytime soon.

"Right." Patricia tapped her fingers on her desk. "Unfortunately, I have to let you go."

My entire body froze. "Um, what?"

She pinched her lips together and then relaxed them as she shrugged. "I just don't think that this is working between us."

I blinked as my brain tried to process what she was saying. "It's not working?"

She nodded. "Yes. It's time to call it quits."

"Why?" tumbled out of my lips before I could stop it.

Patricia blinked as she pulled back a bit. As if my outburst startled her. "Let's not make a scene."

Anger. Frustration. Rage. Emotions were rising up inside of me, and I wanted to scream. I wanted to cry. I wanted a hole in the ground to open up and swallow me. This wasn't what I needed right now. Not after my phone call with Miles and my impending trip back down memory lane.

I needed this job. I needed to have something to come back to when I was in the hellhole that was my past.

Coming back to no job and unpaid bills was not going to ease anything I was going to face in the immediate future.

"It's just time for you to move on. I hope you can respect my decision and leave with grace." She reached out and grabbed her readers next to her computer and slipped them on. Then she turned back to the computer and began typing.

I sat there, trying to force myself to stand. Trying to force my muscles to move. I needed to thank her, walk out of the room, and pack up my desk with grace. But I was stuck in quicksand as the stress of what she said consumed me. The decision had already been made, and I couldn't do anything to stop it. It was the night I was rushed to the emergency room all over again.

The absence of a heartbeat as the nurse desperately tried to find it as she ran the wand across my stomach.

The pain.

The loneliness.

The sound of Patricia's intercom ringing snapped me out of my thoughts as she leaned forward and said, "Michelle, call security. We may have an issue."

I blinked a few times to pull myself from my stupor. Even though my ears were ringing, I forced myself to push my memories from my mind and focus. "No, it's fine. I'm leaving," I rasped as I stood and crossed the room.

Even though all of my southern upbringing told me to turn around and thank her, I ignored it. Instead, I pushed open the door and headed out into the lobby, where I felt Michelle's stare on my back as I waited for the elevator.

I needed to get out of there. I needed to breathe.

When the doors slid open, I kept to the corner as I pressed the button and waited for the doors to close and silence to engulf me. I hunched forward, taking deep breaths as I tried to calm the pounding of my heart.

Once I was back on my level, I hurried over to my office and shut the door. I didn't have much, so I just shoved my belongings into my purse. I logged out of my programs and then powered off my computer.

"You got fired?" Sara's voice pierced through the silence.

I glanced up at her and then nodded and focused on clearing out my desk drawer.

"Why?"

I shrugged, hating that she was asking me these questions. My emotions were about to boil over, and the last thing I needed was for anyone at this company to see the pain I was in. "I don't know." I sighed as I paused and looked around. "And I don't care. It's about time I went out on my own, anyway. I've done enough to realize that I can do this for myself."

I pursed my lips. "I mean, I probably won't." I shrugged. "But it's nice to know that I have it to fall back on." I pulled my purse strap up onto my shoulder and gave her a smile. "For now, I'm going to head to my hometown to finish up my grandmother's estate, and then I'll see where life takes me after that."

Sara jutted out her bottom lip. "Are you sure you're going to be okay?"

I rounded my desk and stood a foot away from her. I gave her an encouraging smile even though I was dying inside. "I'll be fine." I patted her shoulder. "I'll be great." Then I lowered my gaze to catch hers. "Just make sure that you leave before she changes you. You deserve better."

Sara met my gaze and then nodded. "Okay. I will."

"Promise?"

"Promise."

I patted her shoulder once more and then stepped around her and over to my office door. Once I was in the lobby, my shoes echoed on the floor as I made my way over to the elevator and pressed the button.

The sun hit me as I walked out of the building, the wind whipping around me. I took in a deep breath as I turned to stare up at the glistening office windows above me.

Then I took another deep breath, crossed the court-yard, and climbed into a waiting taxi.

I looked out the window as the driver pulled away from the sidewalk. I kept my gaze focused on the buildings and the pedestrians that passed by us as we drove.

Back in my apartment, I tossed my purse down on my frayed and faded couch and then hurried over to my bath-room where I flipped on the shower.

I needed to wash this day off of me. I needed the feeling of hot water beating down onto my back to clear my mind.

For now, I needed to focus on getting to Harmony and dealing with Gran's inn.

After that, I could freak out.

2

MILES

SWEET TEA &
SOUTHERN GENTLEMAN

I STARED AT MY PHONE, which I'd just half placed, half dropped onto the counter in front of me. Frustration boiled up inside of my chest as I placed a hand on either side of the phone. Then I took a step back and dropped my chin to my chest. I closed my eyes as the conversation with Shelby ran through my mind.

I hated that I had to call. I hated that Charlotte had passed away. I hated how broken this family had become.

Most of all, I hated that even after all of these years, the sound of Shelby's voice made my heart change cadence.

It was a ridiculous reaction, especially when she was the one who'd left. She was the one who had walked away. Sure, I'd let her go. After all, what could I do? She'd had that determined fire in her gaze, and after being burned a few too many times, I learned to get out of her way.

But now, standing in the kitchen of Harmony Inn, I cursed myself for not being stronger. I was going to have to face her once more. If I had tried to fix what had broken so long ago, maybe I wouldn't feel so anxious. If only I had enough courage to explain why I pushed Clint away like I did, I might not be here right now. But the night I walked in on Clint with Winnie and told him to shape up or ship out, I'd never expected that he would take the latter option. I thought he'd do the right thing by Shelby and stop sleeping around.

I'd been wrong.

I will never forget the anger in her eyes as she stared at me. I wanted a chance to explain myself, but she never gave it to me. I feared that bringing her back here once more was going to be as pleasant as sticking my hand into the cage of a hungry lion. Unpredictable and would most likely leave me missing a limb.

"This is going to be a disaster," I muttered under my breath.

"I-sas-er," echoed next to me.

I glanced over to see Belle sitting in her highchair. Her hair was slicked back from the cereal milk she was now wearing. Fruit Loops dotted her clothes and the floor, and her bowl was turned over, creating a milk ocean in her tray. Despite looking like a complete mess, she grinned up at me.

"That's right, Belle," I said as I grabbed a clean dishrag

from the drawer next to me and flipped on the warm tap water. "This is a disaster."

Belle shrieked with laughter and began slapping the milk puddle on her highchair tray. That caused me to quicken my pace to clean her up before the whole kitchen became a milk Chernobyl.

It took some wrangling, but I finally got her out of the high chair and wiped down. She puttered around the kitchen, opening cupboard doors, while I focused on cleaning the high chair and floor. With everything straightened out, I called for Belle to follow me as I pushed through the kitchen door and out into the inn's dining room.

Breakfast was now over, and it was time for me to clean things up. Charlotte always emphasized how important the guest was, and even though I was still reeling from the events early this morning, there was a sort of calm that came from keeping up with old habits.

Plus, I wasn't ready to face what Monday was going to bring to me. I'd lived the last few years with Charlotte in my everyday life, but I knew I was nowhere near prepared to visit with her granddaughter once again.

A year ago, Charlotte had moved out to the small cottage a few hundred yards from the inn after she broke her hip. It was harder for her to get around, and stairs were out of the question. Plus, there was no way she was going to allow a lift to be installed in the inn because it would ruin the ambiance she was trying to create.

Instead, she forced me to move into the keeper's quarters while she *"took her retirement"* in the new building.

It made her absence not quite as pronounced. But, even after six months of her being gone, I was still struggling with the weight of running this place by myself. Life was harder without her here, and in the sappy moments of my life, I allowed myself to admit that I missed her.

A lot.

"Belle," I called to my daughter. She was pulling on the tablecloth, causing the dishes to slide across the dark oak table.

She giggled and moved to hide under the table. Realizing that I had a small window to actually get some work done before she emerged to wreak havoc once more, I began to gather up the dishes in a grey tub I'd stashed in the far credenza. Once they were picked up, I called for Belle to follow me as I pushed back into the kitchen.

Luckily, she was in a good mood, and a few seconds later, she followed me through the door. It didn't take me long to get the dishes loaded and for the hum of the dishwasher to fill the air. I grabbed a granola bar from the pantry and pulled the wrapper off.

The distraction of cleaning up after breakfast gave me a break from thinking about Shelby. But now that everything was taken care of and Belle was coloring a big blob of purple on the whiteboard I'd installed to keep her from drawing on the walls—my mind returned to our conversation and the will that was going to be read in just a few short days.

That was, *if* she decided to come at all. I picked up my phone from off the counter and glanced down at it. No new messages. No missed calls. She hadn't called back to cancel. I was cautiously optimistic that she might actually come.

"Give it time," I muttered as I slipped my phone into my back pocket, bringing myself back down to reality. I knew better than to get my hopes up. Especially when it came to Shelby.

Belle glanced over at me for a moment before returning to her masterpiece.

I folded my arms and clicked my tongue a few times. Then I closed my eyes and took a deep breath. So many memories flooded my mind, and it was hard to process them all. I wanted to be stronger. I needed to be, for my daughter and for this inn. But I felt like I was failing.

I felt a small hand land on my leg, causing me to open my eyes. Belle was standing in front of me with her eyes wide. I shoved down my feelings and shot her a big smile. "What's up, pumpkin?"

"Daddy sad?" she asked in her small toddler voice.

I knelt down in front of her and pulled her into a hug. "I'm not sad. Not when I have you." I buried my face in her neck and blew a raspberry.

She shrieked and wiggled away before she wrapped her small arms around my neck and squeezed. I held her tight as I stood. When Tamara, my ex, left Belle on my doorstep three years ago, I thought my world had ended. I wasn't the father type. I had issues of my own.

But I couldn't just abandon Belle. Tamara said she was in no condition to raise a child and her future was up to me, and then she left. I went from a bachelor to a father overnight.

Thankfully, Charlotte saw my predicament and gave me a job and a place to stay. Even though her daughter had divorced my father years ago, she still saw me as her grandson. We'd been close before, but after Belle came into our lives, we were like a real grandmother and grandson.

Which was why I had no idea how I was going to make it through the ups and downs of fatherhood without her support. She'd been my rock, and with her gone, I was alone.

Realizing that I was spiraling, I pushed away my pain and pulled back, glancing down and giving Belle a big smile. "Wanna go for a ride in the car?" I asked as I hoisted her up.

She giggled and nodded, gripping onto my shirt as I bounced her a few times.

I locked up the small office off the side of the kitchen and left a note at the front desk for the guests. The only guests we currently had were an older couple who were here visiting their kids and a business man who spent most of his time in town. I let them know I was out and that they could call me if they needed anything.

Once Belle was buckled in her car seat, I climbed behind the wheel and started up the truck. I needed to go somewhere or I was going to go mad.

My gaze drifted over to Charlotte's cottage as I drove past it. My throat tightened, and I cleared it as I focused my attention back onto the road in front of me. Belle needed me to be her rock, and that started with me getting my crap together.

Truth was, I'd known that Charlotte would pass away eventually. She'd been ninety-three and had numerous health issues. I just never thought that it would *really* happen. She was such a force in my life that death never seemed like an option for her.

Until it was.

I blinked a few times with the inn in my review mirror, clarity returning. Even though *I'd* never emotionally prepared for Charlotte's passing, she had. Her only regret, one that she mentioned on numerous occasions, was her relationship with Shelby.

I drummed my fingers on the steering wheel as Belle's preschool songs blared on the radio. She was holding her doll by one arm and staring out the window as she bobbed her head to the beat. I smiled as I brought my attention back to the road.

Once we got into downtown Harmony, I zeroed in on Godwin's grocery store. Belle was almost out of applesauce, and there was no way I wanted to be on the receiving end of her temper tantrum if we ran out.

I pulled into the nearest parking spot and turned off the engine. Once Belle was out of her seat and into the shopping cart, we took off toward the sliding doors. Cool air conditioning washed over me as I pushed inside. It was busy for midmorning on a Friday.

Betty Godwin was running the only open register. She looked up when I came in and gave me a wide smile.

I nodded in her direction as I pushed the cart into the produce section.

"Let me know if you need anything, Miles," she called after me.

I raised a hand to let her know I heard her, but kept my focus forward. It wasn't until I was down the cereal aisle that Belle started to get cranky, so I used my elbows to steer the cart so I could peel her a banana.

"Ow," a soft feminine voice followed the cart's sudden halt.

I straightened and glanced up to see a woman, not much younger than me, standing there, rubbing her ankle. Heat pricked the back of my neck as I shot her a sheepish look. "I'm so sorry," I said as I handed the banana to Belle. "She was desperate. I should have parked this thing instead of multitasking."

The annoyed look in the woman's eyes faded as she glanced over at Belle and then back to me. She shook her head. "And I was too focused on which cereal to buy to realize I was standing in the wrong lane."

I glanced around the aisle. "Wrong lane?"

"You know." She moved her hands in each direction like a stewardess signaling where the exits were.

"Ah." Then I chuckled. "I guess I've never adhered to the rules of the road here at Godwin's."

Her smile was soft as she shrugged.

I glanced around. "Are you new here? I've never seen you around." And then I felt stupid. That sounded like an extremely cheesy pickup line. Which was ridiculous because I was in no shape to date anyone.

She nodded. "I'm here visiting my aunt."

"Your aunt?" I furrowed my brow. "Who's your aunt?"

She reached out and pulled a box of Raisin Bran down from the shelf. "Betty Lou Thompson."

I nodded. "I know Miss Thompson. She tried to swindle me into buying her antique table set." I leaned forward. "I know a knockoff when I see one."

The woman dropped her jaw as her eyes widened. Her eyes sparkled as she let out a soft gasp. "Are you calling my aunt a swindler?"

Heat warmed my cheeks. "No, no..." I swallowed. "That's not what I meant."

The woman chuckled as she stepped closer to me. "That's okay. I once found an IKEA sticker in her garbage, so..."

I quirked an eyebrow. "Really?"

She pinched her lips together and nodded as she pulled back. "But you didn't hear it from me." Then she pretended to lock her lips.

"Mum's the word," I said as I brought my finger to my lips.

A silence fell between us, but neither of us moved. I wasn't sure what I was doing. I had no interest in dating anyone right now. But there was something about being noticed by a woman that had me glued to my spot. My life had become taking care of Belle and the inn. I was slowly losing myself and the things that I liked.

I wanted to feel like a man again, and the way this woman was looking at me made my heart pound in my chest.

"I didn't catch your name other than you're Miss Thompson's niece."

She dropped her box of Raisin Bran into her basket and then stepped forward, extending her hand. "Laura Smith," she said.

I took her hand. Her skin was soft and warm, and it shocked me. It had been years since I'd touched a woman...and I missed it. "Miles Lachlan," I replied when she raised her eyebrow as if she were expecting a response.

"It's nice to meet you, Miles." She slipped her hand from mine, and then I felt stupid when I realized I hadn't let it go. Luckily, she had already turned her attention to Belle. "And who is this?"

Belle was halfway through eating her banana, but the

sudden attention from a stranger had her lifting her arm up and shielding her face. She turned her body away from Laura.

"This is Belle," I said when Laura turned to look at me. Her eyes were wide with worry, and I didn't want her to think she'd done something wrong. "She's my suddenly shy daughter." I reached out to poke Belle in the rib. She squirmed but remained hidden.

"Oh, your daughter?" Laura asked, her gaze dropping down to my ring finger.

"I'm not married," I blurted out. Then I mentally punched myself. Might as well have *loser at love* tattooed on my forehead.

Laura met my gaze and smiled. "Ah," she said. Then she leaned closer. "Neither am I."

There was a softness to her features and a look in her eye that got my heart racing. I raised my eyebrows, not sure what to say. And then, "Oh, nice," emerged before I could police it.

Laura giggled and straightened. "Maybe two unattached people can meet up for drinks sometime?"

I wanted to say yes. I wanted a night away from the inn. To feel like myself once more. But I knew that was a pipe dream. I was a father and a business owner. I didn't have time for dating.

"I'm super—"

Laura held up her hand. "Don't finish that sentence." She set her basket down on the floor and opened her purse. "Here's my business card. If you decide that you're tired of saying no, give me a call. I'm around for the week and would love to help you relieve some stress." Her gaze raked down my body. "Whatever that might take."

My brain fell into autopilot. Somehow, I managed to grab her card, slip it into my back pocket, mutter something halfway intelligible, and head down the aisle without much thought.

Once I rounded the corner, I blew out my breath. Belle had emerged from her hiding place and was staring at me. I was pretty sure she had no idea what had just happened, but I couldn't help but feel like she was judging me. I squeezed the shopping cart handle with both hands and rolled my shoulders.

It had been a while since any woman had shown me that kind of attention. Once I moved in with Charlotte, most of the women I talked to were silver haired. They always told me, "I have a granddaughter I'd love for you to meet."

But to be here, in Godwin's of all places, flirting with a woman?

It shook me.

"All done," Belle said as she dropped the rest of her banana, which had turned to mush, onto the ground.

I snapped out of my trance a little too late as I dove for the food, but it hit the floor before I could stop it. I growled as I picked it up and searched for a garbage, reality hitting me in the face.

This was why I didn't date. This was why I avoided the opposite sex. My life was too complicated. There was no way a woman would want to walk into this mess. If I didn't even know how to sort my own crap out, how was I going to bring someone else into it?

The business card felt like a brick in my back pocket as I finished up my shopping and headed for the checkout lane. Thankfully, I didn't run into Laura while Betty rang up my items. I focused my attention on bagging them as she pushed them down the conveyor to me. When I was all rung up, I took the receipt and bid her farewell.

Once Belle and the groceries were safely packed into my truck, I returned the cart and climbed into the driver's seat. I slammed the door and gripped the steering wheel in front of me, vowing that when I got home, I was going to toss Laura's business card.

Dating and I had never mixed in the past, and I was fairly certain we wouldn't mix well now.

I was never going to find love again.

3

ABIGAIL

THE SOFT MORNING breeze played with the hem of my skirt as I stood in front of the bookstore, rifling through my purse for my keys. I felt a yawn coming on, so I paused and allowed it to happen.

Baby Samuel had been up all night, and I was exhausted.

Sabrina had come into my room the night before, begging me to take my nephew. She needed one night of sleep, and she was ready to pay me a million dollars if I granted it to her. It wasn't hard to say yes. I loved my nephew with all my heart. He was two months old and cuter than ever—but he was loud and cranky. And he kept me up half the night.

"Coffee," I cheered as I pulled my keys triumphantly from my purse and held them up in the air. A random passerby startled and moved closer to the road, obviously avoiding me.

I shot him a sheepish smile as I slipped the key into the lock and turned.

The bookstore was quiet—which it always was. The smell of old paper mingled with the cinnamon wax melt that I had plugged in an outlet in the back room and filled my nose as I took in a deep breath.

"This is heaven," I said to myself as I let the door shut behind me and flicked on the lights. They blinked a few times before relenting and finally turning on all the way.

I clicked the lock back into place and then headed to the back room. After stuffing my purse into the drawer of my desk, I shook my mouse to make my computer wake up. As the old machine creaked to life, I grabbed a scrunchie I'd slipped onto my George Washington bust and pulled my hair back into a low ponytail. I had a few hours before the store would open, and I was determined to get my tax documents together.

"Death and taxes," I said, glancing over at George Washington. He had eyes that looked like he was staring at you no matter where you were in the room. I sighed. Without Sabrina here, I was lonely.

Dad was married and living in Magnolia with Penny. Sabrina had baby Samuel. And I? Well, I had George. But he was only three inches high and made of marble.

"I'm a loser," I said as I plopped down on my desk

chair and pushed back and forth a few times, the wheels creaking as I moved.

I grabbed my phone and stared at my home screen. It was a newborn picture of Samuel wearing a 1920's newspaper boy outfit. He looked so dapper, and for a moment, I missed that screaming little devil. Until another yawn came on. I clicked the side button, and the screen went dark.

"Time to focus, Abigail," I said as I pulled myself up to my computer and brought my fingers to the keyboard.

Two hours later, I was pulling a dozen chocolate chip cookies out of the oven when there was a soft knock on the door. I glanced up to see that it was Missy Hodges, the owner of Apple Blossom B&B and the town's gossip. I groaned but forced a smile, thankful that she couldn't hear my reaction. Her eyes were flitting all over the place, and I wasn't sure I was ready for that kind of energy this early on a Friday morning.

She looked like she was sitting on a golden egg of gossip and I was going to be the first to hear about it.

Wanting to prolong the inevitable, I lifted the cookie sheet into the air so she could see what I was doing—to which she nodded—and I proceeded to take my time moving them to a cooling rack with a spatula. Once they were settled, I started the coffee machine, wiped my hands on my apron, and then headed to the front door and unlocked it.

Missy didn't wait for me to open it all the way. She

hurried inside while I changed the sign to *Open*, and then I turned to see her standing inches from me. Her blue eyes were wide.

"Good morning, Missy," I said as I tucked the few loose hairs that had fallen from my ponytail behind my ear and took a step back.

"Good? Is it really good?"

The panic in her voice startled me. "Isn't it?" I asked.

She took in a deep breath. "Well, I don't know, I just heard that Charlotte Cane indicated that she wanted her *granddaughter* at the will reading on Monday." Missy was heading toward the cafe counter, so I had to quicken my pace to catch up with her.

She was muttering under her breath, and I was already confused about what she'd just spouted off. I didn't want to miss any clues to why she was so worked up.

"Um, what?" I asked as I slipped behind the counter so I could fill up a coffee for her. I wanted to read her lips to make sure I caught every word.

Missy closed her eyes and pressed her hand to her stomach. She took in a deep breath. "I was on my way here, like I always am." She slowly opened her eyes, and her stare made me pull back slightly. "That's when I ran into Merigold, you know, Tom's wife?"

I nodded as I slowly grabbed a to-go cup for her coffee —even though I didn't really know who Tom or Merigold were. But I feared if I asked, she'd take me down a rabbit hole. Until someone provided me with a tangible family tree, I was never going to figure out how people were related to each other in this town.

"Merigold normally has that pink undertone to her skin like she's just gone to the beach, but we all know that woman doesn't do a lick of work or ever go outside." Missy narrowed her eyes before she sighed. "Anyway, I digress. She looked so pale that I had to ask her what was wrong." Missy stopped and stared at me. "You know, so I could help her if something was wrong." She raised her hand toward the sky, and I half expected a *hallelujah* to come from her lips.

I kept busy, shooting her a small smile of acknowledgment. We both knew that she hadn't asked so she could help Merigold. "Of course." Then I paused. "And you're so sweet to think of her."

Missy seemed to like that compliment. "It's only right," she said as she leaned both arms on the counter. "Poor woman couldn't keep it in. She said Charlotte Cane's will reading is going to be a packed house." Missy dropped onto the barstool next to her while grasping her hands and worrying her lips.

It was no secret that Missy and Charlotte had a rivalry. Both were in the hospitality business, Charlotte owning Harmony Island Inn and Missy owning Apple Blossom B&B. And they weren't shy about their distaste for each other, though when they were together, they smiled and laughed like lifelong friends.

I paused as Missy's words washed over me. I hadn't known Charlotte very well. She kept to herself at the inn while her grandson, Miles, ran her errands. Plus, I didn't really run with the over-seventy crowd here on Harmony Island—in fact, I didn't really run with *any* crowd.

I kept to myself and my sister, and that was about it. The last person I opened up to was Naomi, and she worked here for a few days before she was whisked back to Magnolia Island, where all of my friends now lived. Dad and Penny set up a life there. And Penny's daughter, Maggie—my stepsister—and I were close, but we had different lives.

I just wished I could have what Maggie had in Magnolia. A group of women who took care of each other. Here, I didn't have that. And I was beginning to wonder if I ever would.

My gaze made its way back to Missy, who was staring at me. Her methodical blinking made me realize that she was waiting for me to respond. I probably looked like an idiot, standing there, dozing off when she just told me that...well, I still wasn't so sure what the problem was.

"It's a bad thing that her granddaughter is coming to the reading?" I asked as I grabbed a rag from the small sink in front of me and began wiping down the counter. "Isn't that normal?" Besides Mom, I didn't have too much experience with death. My grandparents passed when I was a kid, but I wasn't part of settling their estate.

Missy's blinking turned rapid, and she leaned back like I'd just slapped her. Then she sighed and shifted her weight, sipping her coffee. "Of course, it's bad." She pinched her lips together as if she were trying to form the words that I could see brewing in her mind. My lack of indignation seemed to have startled her.

I quirked an eyebrow at her comment, waiting for her explanation. She stared hard at me for a moment, hinting to the fact that what she wanted to say wasn't exactly churchgoing. She leaned back and clicked her tongue. "I'm just thinking about what Charlotte would want. That house needs to go to someone who *wants* to take care of it."

I studied her. "And that's not her granddaughter?" I figured most of the regal homes on Harmony Island went to the family members. At least, that would explain the intermingling of families here.

Missy's eyes widened, and for the first time, I realized there was so much more to this story than I knew. Most people here had skeletons in their closets, but besides the passive-aggressive way they spoke to each other, they never really opened the door wide enough for any of them to slip out.

This was a skeleton in Harmony's closet, and I was fairly certain Missy had no intention of letting me know the details.

Her lips fluttered, but I really wasn't interested in playing *pick around the words to find the actual meaning*. The bookstore was going to open in just a few minutes, and most of the construction workers in town came to my front door for breakfast every morning. If I was going to be ready for them, I needed to finish stocking my shelves.

"I'm sorry that she's coming to town. I hope that the will reading will go smoothly and everyone will be happy." I prayed my wide smile and soft gaze would calm Missy down. But the furrow between her brows remained.

"Yeah," she mumbled as she slung her purse over her shoulder and grabbed her cup of coffee. "I doubt that, but I appreciate your words."

I nodded before focusing my attention on rinsing out the rag. "Well, if I hear anything once she gets here, I'll let you know."

Missy turned to look at me. I could see the wheels turning in her head as she nodded. "And I will let you know if I hear anything as well."

"I'm sure you will," tumbled out before I could stop it. I clamped my lips shut and glanced up at her to see that she'd knitted her eyebrows together. There was no way that I wanted to get on her bad side. "Because you're such a sweetheart, making sure everyone knows what's going on in this town." My smile felt sickly sweet as I kept it plastered to my face. Missy studied me for a moment before her smile returned.

"If I didn't, half the town wouldn't know what's going on."

"Exactly."

She took a sip of her coffee. "Well, I should go. I've got things to do at the B&B."

I nodded. "Of course. See you tomorrow?"

She waved at me. "As always."

The jingle of the bell on the door marked her departure. With her gone, I let out my breath as I leaned forward and rested my elbows on the countertop. I rubbed my temples and closed my eyes, Missy's words running around in my mind.

Charlotte Cane's granddaughter was coming? Even though I didn't know the situation, if Missy was this concerned, then this granddaughter was going to shake up the town. Which might not be a bad thing.

I drummed my fingers on the counter just as the door opened and a group of construction guys made their way inside. They looked out of place as they stood there, glancing around.

I grabbed my order pad and waved them over. "You guys looking for some coffee?"

They looked relieved as they headed in my direction. "We sure are," the tall one with a greying beard said as he gave me a quick wink. "And maybe some of those delicious smelling cookies?"

There was a collective mumble of agreement from the other men.

Grateful for the distraction from my thoughts, I jotted down their orders and got started. At least if Harmony Island was about to be shook up, the bookstore would remain unscathed. With all the uncertainty of the past, I was going to rely on the things in my life that were normal.

Normal didn't seem that bad anymore.

4

SHELBY

SWEET TEA &
SOUTHERN GENTLEMAN

I STARED at the suitcases strewn across my bed. Half of the clothes in my closet had been pulled out and were either draped over my bed frame, on the chair in the corner of my room, or they were hanging from the open drawers of my dresser.

It wasn't until this very moment that I doubted my choice in fashion. Everything I owned seemed too fancy for Harmony—which meant I was going to stick out. There was a part of me that thought that wasn't a bad thing. I needed my old hometown to know I'd been successful—even though I was currently unemployed.

But I couldn't let them know that. Not when everyone had seemed so sure that little Shelby Sorenson would never amount to anything.

Growing up, I had been all the statistics. Dating the town's bad boy? Check. Pregnant senior year? Check.

Drunken accident that changed the course of my life?
Double check.

I can still remember the town busybodies sitting on the
black iron patio furniture at the Sunny Side Up Diner,
sipping on their iced tea and saying things—without actually saying things—as I passed by.

"Look. Look, look."

"Honey, I see her."

"Did you hear?"

"Yeah, I heard. Bless her soul."

"And so young."

"Mmhmm."

"I was going to bring her a Bible last week. Darn shame
I didn't. It may have helped."

"Aww, you're such a sweetie. And it would have
helped. I know it."

"Mmhmm."

The weight in my stomach spread throughout my
entire body, making me feel weak. I pushed aside the
clothes on my chair and collapsed on the plush velvet
cushions.

When I woke up this morning, the events of yesterday
seemed like an awful dream. I even got ready for work. But
then I emptied my purse to put my lunch in it and found
all of my desk belongings.

That's when the memory of what had happened
washed over me. I was heading to Harmony Island for the
reading of Gran's will. And I was jobless.

I spent a good portion of the morning crying in the bathtub while eating ice cream and surrounding myself with bubbles, until I forced myself to get dressed and start packing. I was planning on leaving tomorrow morning, and there was no way I could walk into the minefield of what Gran was going to ask me to do unprepared.

I needed to look successful, high-powered, and determined—even if it was all a lie.

It was the only way I was going to keep my sanity.

"I'm an idiot," I whispered as I covered my eyes with my arm and allowed the darkness to seep into my soul.

The sound of my doorbell ringing caused me to drop my arm and stare up at the ceiling. I wasn't in the mood for visitors, and it wasn't like I had many friends. I wasn't rich enough to run with the socialites, and everyone around me was hustling like I was. With the cost of rent here, work was all any of us did.

Whoever was pressing the doorbell picked up speed. Realizing they weren't going to stop, I pushed off the chair and made my way out to the hallway.

"I'm coming. I'm coming," I said as I unlocked the door and pulled it open.

Charity, my cousin, was standing in the dimly lit hallway. Her cheeks were pink, and she was in her running clothes. Her ponytail was windblown, and her blue eyes were bright as she stared at me.

"Took you long enough," she said as she pushed past me into my living room.

I sighed. My cousin was the only person I knew when I moved here. She was from my dad's side, which was why I reached out to her when I packed up my lone suitcase and drove my twenty-year-old car from Harmony to New York City. We roomed together until she got married. But that relationship only lasted a few months, and by the time she kicked him to the curb, I had found my own place.

That didn't stop her from unexpectedly dropping in every now and then. Most times, if she was visiting, she needed something.

"Come on in," I said, shutting the door and turning to see her slip her shoes off and head for the kitchen. "Did you run here?" I asked as I followed her.

She opened the fridge as I rounded the corner, and I watched her take a quick scan of the inventory—which was meager at best. "No bottles?" she asked, flicking her gaze up to meet mine.

We were in different tax brackets. Even though I was hustling to climb the income ladder, she preferred to date her way up. The last thing I'd heard, she was dating some Duke I'd never heard of.

"Tap water is just fine," I said, to which she wrinkled her nose.

"This is why your life isn't doing better." She wiggled her finger in the air as if to indicate that she was talking about my entire body.

"My life needs me to drink incredibly expensive bottled water to thrive?"

She sighed and brought her newly manicured finger-nails to her temples. "No, no." Then she breathed out while muttering under her breath, "The things I have to teach." Her smile widened as she glanced over at me. "What you wear, drink, buy." She waved at my apartment. "Where you live...it matters."

I tried not to roll my eyes. "Why would it matter? I'm good at what I do. And I'm pretty sure that Cosmo wouldn't write an article about New York's rising wedding planner if they cared about that kind of stuff."

Charity looked confused before recognition passed through her gaze. "That photo of your boss where you were in the background?"

Heat burned my cheeks. Sure, the article was about Patricia, but I was in the photo. My face was in a magazine that was in every American home. That had to count for something.

Charity snorted as she pulled out her phone from the tiny pocket of her yoga pants. "You haven't seen the story, then," she said as she swiped her finger on the screen a few times and held it up for me to see.

"See what?" I asked, but then I saw the title of the arti-cle, "*New York's First Daughter, Willow Parks, to Take Job at Elite Wedding Planner Inc.*" My stomach sank. "What?" I asked, grabbing her phone and staring at the words just to make sure I hadn't read it wrong.

"Yep," Charity said.

The whole world spun around me. That's why

Patricia fired me. It was all so she could hire Willow. My face must have paled, because suddenly, Charity had both hands on my upper arms and was guiding me to the only kitchen chair I had.

"Sit down and let me get you some water," she said. Or at least, I think that's what she said. My ears were ringing and my head felt cloudy.

When she returned, she uncurled my fingers from her phone and set the cold glass in my palm. When I didn't move my fingers to hold it, she did it for me.

"Anything you want to tell me?" she asked as she started doing some yoga stretches in the middle of my kitchen floor.

I sighed and set the glass down before I leaned forward and collapsed on my forearm. "My life is in the crapper," I whispered.

"So, you got fired."

I moaned and nodded but didn't move to face her.

Charity clicked her tongue. "That witch."

I sighed, lifting my shoulders as I drew in my breath. "This sucks."

Charity was quiet for a moment before suddenly standing up and punching me.

It startled me enough to make me sit up and grip my arm where she'd hit me. "What the—"

"Stop it." She was a foot in front of me, looking down at me with a meaningful stare.

"You hit me," I said as I drew my eyebrows together.

"Your aura is messed up enough as it is. All this negative energy you're putting out there, it needs to stop." She took a step back and began to stretch again.

I stayed upright, rubbing my arm as I continued to glare at her.

"Your face will freeze like that," she said without looking over at me.

I pumped my eyebrows up and down a few times to release the tension. It didn't help. I was stressed. Not only about this, but also about Harmony Island.

I threw my hands up and let my arms fall to my side. "What do you suggest I do?"

Charity stood, crossed her arms, and rested her hip against the counter. She studied me for a moment and then clicked her tongue. "Go out with Titan."

I blinked. Was she speaking another language? "What?"

She had her phone in her hands and was already typing away with her thumbs. "Titan Strom. He's the linebacker I dated last month. He's single, and I'm sure he's up for something fun."

I held up my hand as if that was going to stop her—it didn't. Her fingers kept flying, so I took a step toward her. "Charity, hold up."

She shook her head. "If you don't get out in front of this, it could kill any chance you have for a future business here. If you don't make a mark—even if it's fake—then you'll be forgotten. You need to stay relevant in the eyes of every bride and future bride in New York." I placed my hand on the screen, but her fingers had already stopped. "I sent it."

I blinked. My brain still playing catch up. "You what?"

"I asked him if he wanted in."

"In on what?"

She nodded toward me. "You."

The floodgates opened. I stammered for a few seconds before I found my way to the kitchen chair and sat down again so I could rest my head in my hands. "I can't date Titan. I can't date anyone. I'm heading to Harmony tomorrow for the reading of Gran's will."

"Oh."

I took in a deep breath as I tried to silence the anxiety rushing through my mind. A ping from Charity's phone caused me to look over at her. She was staring down at the screen with her eyes wide.

"What did he say?" I asked before I could stop myself.

She shook her head and slipped her phone into her pocket. "It's not a big deal. You said no."

Even though I wasn't ready to process what all of this meant, I knew it would be foolish to leave for Harmony without at least something to come back to.

"Did he say yes?" I asked, forcing my confidence to the surface.

She pursed her lips and nodded. "He said he's game."

I furrowed my brow as I let her plan stew in my mind. It wasn't going to be real, but it would appear real enough for the next week or so. And that was all I needed. A little time to process Charlotte's death and figure out a plan to stay relevant in New York's wedding world.

If I was in Charity's place and she was faced with this seemingly impossible situation, I would suggest this temporary plan as well. So why was I saying no?

I drummed my fingers on the table. I narrowed my eyes. "Can he meet me at Java House in two hours?"

Charity shrugged. "I can ask him."

I nodded, grateful for the distraction. I already knew what outfit I was going to wear and how I was going to style my makeup. If I was going to portray that we were dating and that I had found the man I wanted the world to know I loved, I needed to look the part.

"Perfect. Tell him to meet me there at eleven, if he's in." I stood and was across the room before Charity called out to me.

"What about the will reading?"

I waved her question away. "I'll be heading to Harmony tomorrow. And you're right, it's better to have something fake in the works than nothing at all." I turned and gave her a wide smile. "Thanks for looking out for me."

She let out a *psssh* and shrugged. "I've got your back."

I smiled and nodded. "While I'm gone, you have free rein with my apartment. Make it look..." I waved my hand in her direction. "Social media ready."

She laughed and nodded. "Will do. It'll be a fun makeover."

I winced, worried what my credit card bill would be once she was done, but I pushed it from my mind. It was all for the cause. Not only did I need to prove myself to New York society, but I wanted to prove to the women on Harmony Island that I did make something of myself. That I didn't need their pity.

I was Shelby-freaking-Sorenson and that meant something.

5

SHELBY

SWEET TEA &
SOUTHERN GENTLEMAN

THE SMELL of coffee and espresso assaulted my nose as I pulled the door to Java House open and stepped inside. The morning rush was over, and there were only a few stragglers in line waiting to place their order. In the wee hours of the morning, the line was always out the door, so I was grateful for the lack of people.

The bell on the door chimed as it shut behind me. A man, wearing a beanie and sitting at a nearby table, turned to look at me for a moment before dropping his gaze back to his phone. I took in a deep breath as I hugged my purse to my chest and hurried to slip into an empty booth.

I had to talk myself into coming about twenty times before the rideshare driver dropped me off in front of this coffee house, and then I had nowhere else to go but inside. My bags were packed and waiting for me just inside my apartment door. When I finished up here, I was going to drown myself in chocolate and chick flicks before I packed the back of my car and left in the wee hours of the morning.

"Shelby?" a deep gravelly voice asked, startling me.

I yelped and turned to see a huge man standing just a foot away from me. His t-shirt was stretched to its limit over his bulging muscles. He was tan, and his very blond hair looked bleached against his skin. His smile was wide as he stuck out his gigantic hand.

"Titan?" I asked, my voice coming out a whisper. His parents named him accurately.

He nodded, and just as I began to raise my hand to meet his, he reached down and closed the gap. "Nice to meet you," he said as his hand literally engulfed mine and half my forearm. He dropped my hand and turned to slide into the bench across from me. "You're cute," he said as he leaned back against the booth and gave me a wink.

My mind was still trying to play catch up, and something that sounded like a giggle escaped before I clamped my hand over my mouth and stared, mortified, at him.

He quirked an eyebrow, smiled, and continued chewing the gum I could see rolling around his extremely white teeth.

Thankfully, I composed myself enough to remember why he was here and what I was going to ask him to do. "Thank you for meeting with me. I'm not sure how much Charity told you—"

"Is this a business meeting?" Titan interrupted me.

I startled and stared up at him. "Um, what?"

He nodded toward my fingers, which were threaded through each other and both of my hands were resting on the table in front of me.

"It's not a business meeting," I said, pulling my hands apart and letting one fall on my lap.

He wrinkled his nose. "You just look like you're about to ask me for money or something." He leaned forward. "Which I don't do anymore."

I waved away his comment. "I'm not looking for money." I took in a deep breath, although asking for a loan seemed infinitely less embarrassing than asking him to pretend to date me. "Did Charity say that I needed money?" I asked, panic taking over me.

He let out a laugh. It rumbled so loud that it startled the other coffee shop patrons. My cheeks burned, but I forced a smile as well. It was only a matter of time before someone realized that I was sitting with Titan Strom, linebacker for the New York Panthers. Hopefully, they would get nosy and start taking pictures. Rumors would spread, and I would have bought myself a few weeks to let the stories fly.

He shook his head once his laughter died down. "Nah, she didn't say that." He leaned forward and punched my shoulder. "I'm just kidding. I know why I'm here," he said as he leaned back once more, his left leg dangling out from under the table.

Relief flooded my body. I was certain that my cheeks were pink, but I wasn't going to let that stop me from my goal. I needed a fake boyfriend.

"So, you're okay going along with this?"

He studied me for a moment before he shrugged. "What will I get out of it?"

His gaze flicked down to my mouth, and in that moment, I realized I'd started chewing on my lower lip without realizing it. A response to stress that I'd picked up as a kid. I stopped and straightened, clearing my throat. "Er—well, what do you want?" I winced as I anticipated his response.

It probably wasn't wise for me to leave the question so open ended. I'd read some articles recently about Titan, the linebacker player. But with one look at me, he had to know I wasn't the kind of girl that participated in that.

I was far from the perfect blonde cheerleader that he normally dated.

Then I felt stupid. It didn't matter if I wasn't his type. We were here for one purpose and one purpose only—to save my career while I went to deal with my grandmother's estate.

That was all.

"I could plan your future wedding," I offered before he could respond.

He flicked his gaze over at me, his lips tipping up into a smile. "Ain't no woman in this world going to tie this stallion down," he said as he drummed his hands on the table.

Not sure how to respond, I just pinched my lips together and nodded. I had no money—at least not enough to tempt him. If he didn't want my wedding services, what did he want?

He folded his arms across his chest and studied me, like he was sizing me up. I offered him a weak smile, not sure what he was going to say.

Suddenly he cleared his throat, glanced around, and leaned in. "I need a favor."

My eyes widened. Here we go. This was the moment I'd been dreading. "Okay," I whispered.

He studied me. "I need a date to my sister's wedding."

I startled. Why was he asking me when he could ask anyone in the world? "Um, okay."

He nodded toward me. "You're perfect. You're not going to fall in love with me." Then he stopped and leaned closer. "You're not going to fall in love with me, right?"

My cheeks flushed as embarrassment coursed through me. Love was the last thing on my mind. "You don't have to worry about me. I'm not interested in..." I let my words draw out but then waved them away. It was just never going to happen. I was determined to die a single woman, alone and free from heartbreak.

He chuckled as he leaned back. "Which is what I'm looking for. The last thing I need is for some girl to agree to be my fake girlfriend and then sabotage my plans."

I quirked an eyebrow. "Plans?"

It was his turn to blush. He cleared his throat as he

tugged at the collar of his shirt. "Yeah." He sighed. "Long story, but my ex will be at the wedding."

I suddenly had flashbacks of the Carson wedding where the groom's ex showed up with his secret family. The amount of expensive champagne that was thrown that night would make anyone cry.

Of course, it had been my first solo job as a wedding planner, and I'd almost died of embarrassment. Patricia had not been happy, and I thought she would fire me on the spot. But she didn't. Who knew that a year later I'd be here, jobless?

"Why is your sister inviting your ex to her wedding?"

Titan sighed. "It's her best friend. She'll be the maid of honor, and I'm the best man."

I sucked in my breath. "Ouch."

He shrugged. "But if I come with a date, I might make her jealous." He motioned toward me. "Enter you."

I drummed my fingers on the table as I chewed on his words. What was the worst that could happen? It would solidify the impression that Titan and I were together. Plus, I could do some recon work and see what the other planners were doing. There wasn't any harm in checking out your competition. "So, if I agree to go to this wedding with you, we'll be even?"

The smile that emerged was genuine, and it helped melt away some of my stress. He nodded and then shrugged. "It's what I'm looking for; take it or leave it."

It was actually perfect. We could get a few photos of us today, and then I would disappear for a few weeks. Then we'd show up at a wedding together, and that would feed the gossip train long enough for me to launch my business and remain in the tabloids.

I extended my hand across the table. "Deal."

Titan engulfed my hand in his, and we shook on it. Suddenly, he shifted his hand and slipped my fingers between his thumb and forefinger as he leaned forward to press his lips to the back of my hand. Heat permeated my body as I sat there, frozen.

It had been a long time since a man pressed his lips to any part of my body. I'd forgotten what that warmth felt like. My heart pounded in my chest, and I must have been staring at him, because when he pulled back, his eyes widened.

"Was that not okay?" he asked. Then he stopped and stared at me. "Someone has their phone pointed in our direction. If you're planning on slapping me, can you do that once we are alone?" His lips tipped up into a smile that only made my warm body flush even more.

Not sure what to say, I nodded. Thankfully, that movement knocked me out of my stupor, and I was able to focus on the task at hand. I smiled and glanced down, using my embarrassment to my advantage. Hopefully, people would buy that I looked rosy from love and not from shock.

Thankfully, Titan knew how to work the cameras, and in one swift movement he was on my side of the booth, wrapping his arms around me. He smelled incredible and felt so alive as he sat next to me.

I didn't realize until now how much I missed physical touch. Even though my mind was screaming with warning bells, I kept still as he whispered nonsense into my ear for our adoring crowd. I focused on my breathing and on acting the part.

Our session only lasted a few minutes before Titan slipped out of the booth and grabbed my hand. He led the way out of the shop and onto the sidewalk. I didn't think, I just allowed him to guide me over to his convertible, where he held open the door, and I slipped onto the soft, leather seat.

By the time I officially snapped out of my trance, he was driving down the road, tapping his fingers to the music blaring from the radio.

"I think we did pretty good," he yelled over the music and the sound of rushing wind.

I glanced over at him. "Really?"

He nodded. "Although, you're going to have to be less standoffish when we go to the wedding. There's no way Samantha is going to believe that you are completely in love with me." He glanced over and gave me a wink.

"Well, you did kind of spring it on me," I said as I hastily tucked the hair that was flying around my face behind my ears.

"You looked like a nun," he said as he turned his attention back to the road.

I was grateful that his gaze didn't linger. The last thing I needed was for him to keep digging. I didn't want to dredge up my past. I was hours away from facing the very thing I'd run away from. I wanted just a few minutes where I didn't have to think about Harmony, my past, or what my deceased grandmother was going to ask me to do.

I was headed off an emotional cliff whether I wanted to go or not.

"What's your address?" he asked as he waved toward the large screen on the dash.

I punched in my address, and he kept his focus on driving me there. Once he pulled up in front of it, his eyes widened. "This is where you live?" he asked.

I nodded as I pulled open the door. "Yes." Once I stepped out onto the sidewalk, I paused. I wasn't sure what to say. Thanks? You're awesome? I let out a sigh.

"Don't worry, kid," Titan said as he smiled at me. "Our plan will work." He gave me a wink as he pushed the car into gear and merged into traffic.

I stood on the sidewalk, watching him go. Then I turned and faced my apartment, a small glimmer of hope igniting in my stomach. If I could find some peace in Harmony and come back to the future that Titan and Charity were confident was inevitable, then my future was looking brighter.

Although I would always be a cautiously optimistic person, I couldn't help but feel excited.

I was mere weeks away from the freedom that I'd been craving for ten years. And the thought that there was a possibility I could have it...

It made me feel alive for the first time in a long time.

6

ABIGAIL

SWEET TEA &
SOUTHERN GENTLEMAN

FIVE O'CLOCK ROLLED AROUND, and right on time, the front door chimed at Fanny's arrival. I leaned back in my chair, my back popping from the change in position. Fanny was the recently-returned-from-college girl that I'd hired to help run the bookstore at night so I could head home to help Sabrina.

I didn't like turning over control of my shop, but I needed the help because Sabrina needed me. She'd changed after the birth of Samuel, and I worried about her being home by herself, especially at night. During the day, I asked our neighbor, Mrs. Leatherbury to check in on her. And she was good at that. But at night, Mrs. Leatherbury wanted to be home with her husband when he got off work, so I had to make a point of getting out of the bookstore in a timely manner.

It wasn't like Trevor was ever going to show up again. He was long gone, and I doubted he remembered the small town of Harmony and the woman he broke when he left.

"Jerk," I muttered under my breath before forcing a smile and turning to see Fanny standing behind me with her eyebrows raised.

"Jerk?" she asked with a teasing tone.

I pinched my lips together and waved my hand in front of my face. "Just thinking about Sabrina's ex."

Fanny furrowed her brow as she slipped off her jean jacket and draped it on the chair I'd just vacated. "Any particular reason why you were thinking about him?"

I gathered the papers I'd strewn about and tapped them on the counter to straighten them out. "I was up with Samuel all night to give Sabrina a break." I sighed. "What my sister needs right now is the father of her son. But of course, he left without even a goodbye, so I'm stuck being dad to his child."

My eyes widened as my words echoed in my head. "Not stuck." I pressed my fingertips to my lips. "Oh, gosh. That sounded horrible." I squeezed my eyes shut for a moment before opening them again. "I love my nephew, and I'd do anything for him."

Fanny chuckled as she waved away my words. "Girl, I don't fault you for what you said. We love our family members even if it's hard to be around them sometimes." She reached up and began to gather her hair into a high ponytail.

Speaking of families...I leaned toward her. "Guess who was here this morning?"

Fanny finished tying up her hair and ran her hand down her ponytail before focusing on me. "Who?"

"Missy."

She rolled her eyes. "What did the town's gossip want?"

I swallowed, not sure if I should say anything or not, but I needed to tell someone, and I knew Sabrina wouldn't care. So I pushed away the guilt that started to rise in my stomach and continued. "Charlotte's granddaughter is coming to the will reading on Monday." As I said the words, I realized how ridiculous this all sounded.

What seemed like a scandal when Missy said it now just seemed like a random conversation between people making small talk at a coffee shop. Why I thought Fanny would care was beyond me.

Fanny furrowed her brow for a moment. "Oh, really?" she asked, once recognition passed over her face. "That's interesting."

I slammed my hand down on the counter. "See? And from the way Missy was going on, I knew there was something to the story. I just don't know anything about Charlotte, much less her granddaughter who has Missy in such a fit." I blew out my breath as I hoisted myself up onto the counter.

Fanny was studying me. The expression on her face was incredulous.

"So, you know their story?" I asked.

She pinched her lips together.

"Are you going to tell it to me?" I placed my hands behind me and leaned back.

Fanny grabbed the chair and dragged it over so she could sit down. "So, you know Miles?"

I nodded. "He's Charlotte's grandson, right?"

"Step-grandson, er..." She held up a finger. "Ex-step-grandson."

"Ex?"

She nodded. "Miles's dad married Charlotte's daughter. They were married for a few years before they divorced. Charlotte's daughter died, and Miles's dad disappeared. Miles left for about six years until he came back. He moved in with Miss Charlotte, and they ran Harmony Inn together." She let her voice trail off as her eyes sparkled like she was holding in a juicy secret.

I leaned forward, knowing there was something good there. "What?" I asked.

Fanny's eyes widened before she shook her head once more and sighed. "I shouldn't be saying. My momma would be so mad at me for gossiping." She glanced up toward the ceiling before she shook her head once more. "But I guess it's just telling you facts. And that's not gossiping." She paused before she lowered her gaze to meet mine. "Miles has a sordid history with women."

I raised my eyebrows. "Sordid?"

Fanny nodded. "Yes."

"How?" There was no way that Miles had dated Charlotte...was there? "He didn't date..." I let my question disappear as heat permeated my cheeks. I felt wrong discussing this. So what if it was true?

Fanny stared at me for a moment before she covered her mouth with her fingers. "Oh, my gosh, no. Not like that."

I laughed, feeling stupid that my mind went there. I folded my arms and leaned against the counter. "So, if not that, then what?"

Fanny brought her foot up and rested her chin on her knee. "Well, Charlotte's daughter, Emma, had a daughter, Shelby."

"He dated his stepsister?" I asked, feeling like I was hearing the plot to a soap opera.

Fanny shrugged. "It was all town speculation that he liked her, but never anything official. It ended when Shelby started dating Clint."

"Clint?"

"Missy's son."

My eyes widened. "This is getting good."

Fanny nodded. "But Shelby ended up pregnant, and Clint took off. Before they could find him, Shelby lost the baby and left town."

I felt like I needed popcorn and a Coke for this story. My heart was pounding from anticipation.

"Where did he go?"

Fanny shrugged. "No one knows. Or if they do, they don't talk about it."

"Does Missy know where he went?"

"I don't know. Missy doesn't talk about him."

"Huh." Then I paused. "You said he has a sordid past with women. Shelby is one woman."

Fanny nodded as she pulled at the thread of her fraying jeans. "Well, after Miles finally returned, he kind of kept to himself. That was until Tamara moved to town. She was the librarian and had her gaze set on Miles from the get-go."

I chuckled. "You make it sound like she was going to kill him."

Fanny shrugged. "When she left, it was like someone stabbed him in the heart."

"Oh."

"Then Tamara showed up a year later with a baby, claimed it was his, and told him that she couldn't take care of the child anymore."

"Wow." I was surprised that I hadn't heard any of this before, but when I broke it down, it made sense. I mainly kept to myself, and it wasn't like Miles and I were friends. Charlotte had always been pleasant to me, and Missy... well, I doubted she wanted to air her family's dirty laundry to me.

Still, for a small town, it was amazing that everyone had been so tight-lipped about this.

"I'm surprised you didn't know," Fanny said, a small smile on her lips. "It's not every day that I get to tell stories that someone hasn't heard yet."

I jumped down from the counter. "I'm happy to oblige."

"Just keep it quiet that I'm the one who told you. Most people in town don't mess with Missy, and I'd hate for her to find out I was the one talking about her family."

I nodded. "Will do."

I turned to finish cleaning up the counter behind the register when the bell on the front door rang. Fanny came up behind me. "Mind helping him? I gotta run to the bathroom before I clock in."

I glanced over my shoulder to see a man had entered. The sun was streaming in through the picture windows, creating a halo around him and making it hard to see anything but shadow. "Yeah, sure," I said as I straightened my apron and turned to fully greet him.

"Evening," I said as I stepped up to the register. "Are you here for books or food?" I grabbed out a pad of paper and a pencil, already anticipating his answer. Here in Harmony, people rarely came in for books.

"I've never seen a bookstore-slash-cafe before." His voice was smooth and silky. It reminded me of hot chocolate on a cool Christmas evening.

I shrugged. "Books are for pleasure, and the food keeps the lights on."

"Books are for pleasure?" There was a teasing hint to

his voice which sent shivers across my skin. The man stepped toward me out of the sunlight, and my entire body warmed. He was tall, over six foot, and his blond hair was damp like he'd just gotten out of the shower. His clothes were clean, but I could tell he was in a trade because there were black smudges on his shirt and jeans.

"Hi," he said with a smile.

"Hi," I breathed out. Like, no diaphragm work, just air. He must have noticed my reaction because he chuckled before pushing his hand through his damp hair. I was staring, and even though I knew I shouldn't, I couldn't pull my eyes away.

He looked like Hercules had stepped into my tiny store and was standing there in all his god-like glory. His teeth were perfect. His cheekbones could cut glass. And his lips...

I brought my gaze up to meet his, and the edges of his eyes crinkled as he smiled.

"I'd like to order some food..." He peered down one of the book aisles. "Do you have the latest Jackson Richards novel?"

My hands dropped to my sides as my eyes widened. "You like Jackson Richards?"

The mystery man was now leaning one elbow on the counter, smiling at me. "You like him?"

I swallowed and nodded. "Like him? My stepmother is his editor." I waved my hand toward my chest like a fainting woman from one of those old-timey movies. "I met him. And he signed" —I dropped my pad of paper and pencil on the counter and motioned for him to follow me— "all of my books."

Excitement boiled over inside of me as I led him down to the dedicated shelf I'd made for Jackson Richards. In the end, Sabrina said it looked more like a shrine than anything else, but I just shushed her. I loved his books, and the fact that he graciously signed all of my books even though he was going blind meant I was going to make sure I treated his stories with the respect they deserved.

I pulled out Jackson's latest book and handed it over to the mystery man. I tried not to notice how large his hands were as he took it from me. Butterflies erupted in my stomach when I noticed how close he was to me, and I wondered if he'd purposely stood this close. He flipped the book over a few times in his hand.

"Right here," I finally said, lifting up the front cover and the first few pages to reveal Jackson's signature.

"Well, will you look at that," he said as he brought his gaze up to meet mine.

I swallowed. He leaned even closer to me as he ran his finger across Jackson's signature.

"To the Shop Around the Corner," he read, "Jackson Richards." Then he closed the book. "Are you sure you want me to buy this from you?"

I nodded. "Of course. That's what it's here for." I took

it from his hands, but he held on so that we were now holding the book together. I glanced up at him to see him smiling down at me.

"Did you tell me your name?"

I shook my head. My tongue felt twisted in my mouth.

His smile widened. "Do you want to?"

Yes. I did. I'd give him my birthday, my social, my address, even the combination to the safe I've had since I was a kid. Anything to keep him around. It had been so long since I'd been around a man, much less have one look at me like this man was.

The current that was flowing through me from the smell of his cologne and the warmth of his body to his unabashed stare had my head swimming.

"Abigail," I finally managed when my senses came back and I could focus.

"Abigail."

I shivered at the way he said my name. It was like he enjoyed the taste of it on his tongue. My gaze drifted down to his mouth, and suddenly, I was wondering what it might feel like to press my lips to his.

"And yours?" I finally managed to ask through a weak wheeze.

"Anders."

"Anders," I repeated. I wanted to make sure it was seared in my brain. "It's nice to meet you."

"You too." Then his gaze flicked down to my left hand like he was looking for a ring.

"You can just call me Unattached Abigail," I said, hoping that came across less dorky than it sounded in my head.

"Likewise."

"Ha," I said and then pinched my lips. That came out way too loud. "I'm sorry."

He shrugged.

"I'm back," Fanny sang out as she rounded the book-shelf. She stood there with her eyes wide. "I'm—er..." She did a few half-turns as if she were trying to figure out if she should leave or not. "I'm sorry," she finally muttered as she turned her back.

"It's okay, Fanny. Anders here was just picking out a book to buy along with some coffee and food?" I asked, peering up at him.

"Did you make it?"

"Yes," I managed out.

He nodded. "I'll take some food then."

Fanny glanced between us a few times. "Great. What do you want?"

He didn't take his gaze off of me. "Whatever is the town's favorite."

"So, you're not from here?" I asked.

He shook his head. "I'm here for a construction job. The new subdivision off of It'll Do Rd?"

"Ah."

"Hey, my grandma is getting a house there," Fanny piped up.

We both looked over at her as if we suddenly realized that she was still standing next to us.

"Awesome," Anders said.

An awkward silence fell between us. Not wanting to stand here like this, I gave the book that we were still holding a tug and then handed it over to Fanny. "Get him some coffee and a blueberry muffin. And make sure to ring up this book as well."

Fanny nodded and then turned and headed to the cafe.

Now alone, I folded my arms across my chest and smiled at Anders, who was still studying me. "Well, I should go," I said, suddenly remembering that I had Sabrina and Samuel to get home to. Not sure what to say as a farewell, I gave him a smile and started to walk away.

"Hey, Abigail?"

"Yeah?" I turned to see him smile.

"I'll see you around sometime."

I pinched my lips shut and nodded because the only response that wanted to spill from my mouth was a giggle and I was a thirty-year-old woman. I didn't giggle.

Thankfully, I left his presence with some grace, but once I was out of his sight, I turned into Phoebe from *FRIENDS* and ran out of the bookstore to my car. I was still smiling when I walked into the apartment to find an un-showered Sabrina standing in the living room, holding a screaming Samuel.

I immediately took him from her arms and shooed her

off to the bathroom for some alone time while I bounced Samuel. I didn't even mind his wails.

For the first time in a long time, I was happy. For the first time in a long time, I had a *sometime* to look forward to.

I felt...free.

7

SHELBY

SWEET TEA & SOUTHERN GENTLEMAN

IT FELT MORE surreal the closer I got to Harmony Island. It amazed me how much I remembered about the small towns that led up to Harmony and how much things had changed. For a moment, a glimmer of hope swelled in my stomach as I thought that, perhaps, my hometown had changed as well.

But I shot that thought out of my head as soon as it entered. I was just there six months ago. From what I saw when I was out and about, Harmony Island was slowly being dragged into the future kicking and screaming.

I stopped for gas in Powta, a small town with only one stop sign. I didn't want to risk needing gas in Harmony because I had no clue who I was going to run into there. In small towns, every store is a mini meet-up. You never know who you are going to see or what they will want to talk to you about once they corner you.

Getting right to the motel was the most important thing for me right now.

I leaned against Rhonda, my beat-up Corolla, and watched the numbers tick up. I tried not to think about the numbers ticking down in my bank account at the same time. I had no idea how long my account was going to stay positive. Since I didn't know how long I'd be staying here in Harmony, it would behoove me to keep my expenses low.

Just as the pump clicked off, my phone rang. I slipped it out of my pocket and held it between my shoulder and cheek as I pulled the nozzle from my gas tank.

"Hello?"

"Miss Sorenson?"

"Yeah."

"This is Bob at the Harmony Motel."

I nodded and murmured a, "mmhmm," as I waited for my receipt to be printed.

"Well, I have some bad news."

I stopped, my hand on my gas receipt, my brain clearing, and my focus snapping to attention. "What news?"

He cleared his throat. "We've had some plumbing issues. Unfortunately, you won't be able to stay here. Half of our rooms are flooded—"

"And the other half?" My heart was pounding so hard, I could hear it in my ears.

He cleared his throat again. "I'm so sorry that this

might inconvenience your trip, but it's just not possible for you to stay here."

"No, no. That's not going to work for me. I need to stay there."

"I have the numbers for the local inn and the B&B that have said they have space," he continued like he didn't hear the panic in my voice.

I sighed. I knew the other places in town. I just couldn't go there. "That's okay," I murmured as I shoved the receipt into my wallet. I don't know why I took it. They just ended up littering my purse and then my kitchen counter. That decision was a part of the string of wrong decisions I seemed to be making lately. I slipped my phone from my shoulder and gripped it to my cheek, forcing myself to focus. "I'll figure something out."

"I'm truly sorry."

"Not as much as I am," I mumbled before thanking him and hanging up.

I sat in my car, the cool air blasting from the vents and blowing across my skin. My thoughts were rolling around in my mind, and I couldn't settle any of them.

I couldn't stay at the inn, and I certainly couldn't face Missy.

I cursed under my breath as I rested my forehead on my hands gripping the steering wheel. Why did I come here? I should have just told Miles no and hung up.

If I were in New York, I could find a job to tide me over until I could start my own business and try to dig

myself out of the mess that was my life. Just as I was beginning to spiral, my phone went off again. I startled and sat
up. Somehow, it had fallen between my seat and the
center console. I had to shove my hand in hard, but I was
finally able to fish it out.

If it was Bob, there was no way I was going to miss his
call.

"Yes, I'm here. Hello?" I asked as I pushed my hair
behind my ear and settled back in my chair. I held the
phone to my cheek as I waited for Bob's gravelly voice to
tell me that everything was fine with my reservation and
he couldn't wait to see me.

"Shelby?"

My heart sank. Miles. I sighed, my shoulders
slouching and the stinging on my hand becoming more
pronounced. I stretched it out in front of me and saw the
back of my hand was bright pink. "Yeah," I murmured.

"I'm guessing you heard about the motel."

"You heard?"

Miles paused. "Well, yeah. Bob called to let me know
that he was sending his guests to the inn."

"And you assumed that I was staying there."

"Well..."

I closed my eyes and tipped my head back. "I'm not
sure what I'm going to do," I whispered. I hadn't meant for
him to hear it—or how defeated I sounded—but it was out
there now, and he was no doubt chewing on it.

"Shelby, listen, I know it's hard for you to stay here.

But there's a small cottage just a few hundred feet from the inn. You can stay there." His voice dropped. "No memories there."

I swallowed, and the lump in my throat hurt. I hated that I was so weak about this. That any mention of my past, even one so broad, brought tears.

I just wanted to be stronger.

"What do you think?" he finally asked, breaking the thick silence between us.

My mind had wandered, and his words pulled me back. "About what?"

"The cottage. You could stay there as long as you want. No payment necessary."

I chewed on my lip as I squinted out at the setting sun. I wanted to say no. I knew I should. After all, going back to the inn went against the rules I'd mentally set for myself on the drive down. But I had no other choice. Besides, I was already making poor decisions, what was one more?

"I guess."

Silence.

Worried that I'd lost the connection, I pulled my phone from my cheek and glanced down at the screen. The time was still ticking up, indicating that I'd been talking to Miles for over three minutes now.

"Miles?" I asked when I brought the phone back to my ear.

"Yeah, sorry. I guess I just..." He sighed. "I figured you were going to fight me harder about this."

I fiddled with my steering wheel, dragging my hand across the smooth material. "I'm a big girl, Miles. I'm not the same scared child you used to hide in the closet with."

I closed my eyes as my words echoed in my mind. Memories of my mother flying through the house in a fit of drunken rage. Miles grabbing my hand and pulling me into the darkest corner of my closet and burying us both in the laundry on the floor.

When our parents were married, he did a lot for me. That was before Clint. Before the baby. He was responsible for that night. For Clint walking out on me. He may have protected me when we were kids, but my heart was broken because of what he did. And I wasn't sure I could ever forgive him for that.

Miles cleared his throat. "I know you're not a kid anymore, Shelby."

"Good," I hurried to say. I was ready to move on. The past was just that: the past. There was no use digging things back up that were good and buried. "I'm about twenty minutes away. I'll see you at the cottage."

I didn't wait for Miles to say anything. Instead, I hung up and tucked my phone into my purse. After taking a few minutes to do some deep breathing, I started the car and pulled away from the gas pump.

It wasn't long before I took a right down Main Street and headed into downtown Harmony Island. I kept my focus on the road because I'd made memories on each corner of this town.

When I'd been here for Gran's funeral, I'd spent most of the time in my hotel room, drowning myself in work. Now, I had nothing to distract myself with, and that thought caused my chest to feel as if it were collapsing. Breathing was a chore.

Luckily, I made it through town and started down the main drag to the inn without completely panicking and turning around. Soon, the only things that whipped by me were tall trees.

There was something completely calming about driving through the outskirts of Harmony. We were getting closer to the ocean, and even though my air conditioning was on full blast, I could feel the stickiness of the salty air as it surrounded me.

It was so familiar, and despite my efforts, tiny flashes of memory were racing through my mind like a mini movie reel. There were a few good memories of Mom. There were the times Miles and I would run down the beach with sand squishing between our toes. There were even a few high school beach parties that I went to that didn't end in the cops busting us up or Clint passing out in my back seat while Miles and I drove him home.

My childhood wasn't just full of pain, even though that's what rose to the surface when I allowed my thoughts to wander.

I let out my breath as I turned down Whipporwillow Lane and Harmony Island Inn loomed in the distance.

Pain clung to my chest as I methodically took in each breath. I could do this. I could.

I was stronger than I'd allowed myself to believe.

The wraparound driveway led up to the large porch and front door. I chewed my lip as I dropped my gaze and searched the land for the cottage that Miles had mentioned. It didn't take me long to spot it.

I focused my attention on the small, red-sided building and veered off the driveway and down a small paved road.

The cottage was tucked in among the trees that surrounded Gran's property. Even though the yard was full of plants, the grass was cut and the bushes were trimmed. I pulled onto the small slab of concrete on the side of the house and stopped the engine.

I sat for a moment and allowed the darkness that surrounded me to soothe my soul. The sun had dipped well below the trees, the only remaining rays peeking through the tree trunks and spilling soft stripes along the hood of my car.

Not wanting Miles to find me like this, staring at nothing, I pulled the keys from the ignition and dropped them into my purse before I shouldered the strap and pulled on the driver's door.

The hum of crickets and the trill of frogs greeted me. I slammed the car door and slowly turned around.

I was back.

I swallowed as a lump formed in my throat.

I doubted I would ever feel strong here.

The sound of an engine drew my attention over. I didn't have to see his face to know that it was Miles heading to the cottage on a four-wheeler. He bounced a few times as he rode across the yard, and when he saw me staring, he nodded before stopping a few feet in front of me and killing the engine.

After swinging his leg off the seat, he straightened. "Hey," he said.

I nodded, not sure how my voice would sound if I spoke. I wanted to maintain a certain level of dignity on my first night back.

"Hey," was all that came out.

Miles pushed his hand through his hair as his gaze drifted around for a moment before he focused back on me. "How was the drive?"

I shrugged as I gripped the shoulder strap of my purse. "Long. But I managed."

He stared at the ground. "That's good. I'm glad you made it safely." He tipped his face toward the sky as he shoved his hands into the front pockets of his jeans. "I was worried about you."

His words were almost a whisper, and I wondered if I'd heard him right. When he returned his attention to me, he let out his breath and motioned toward the cottage. "I can show you inside."

I nodded and followed after him.

We paused at the front door as Miles unlocked it. I tried not to notice that he stiffened when I neared. We had such a strange relationship, and I wasn't ready to unpack what any of his mannerisms meant. I just wanted to get settled in the cottage and go to sleep.

I was exhausted.

He pushed into the living room, thankfully giving me some space. He walked me through the small kitchen that led to the only bedroom and a small bathroom off the back. I followed after him, making sure to maintain my distance as he told me where everything was.

When we got back into the kitchen, he pulled open the fridge. "I brought you some food from the inn," he said, waving toward the inside.

I dipped down, taking note of the milk, yogurt, and fruit that I could see. "Thanks," I whispered.

"There's breakfast in the dining room every morning." He nodded in the direction of the inn. "I don't mean to brag, but I can make a mean quiche." He smiled before dropping it.

"That's nice," I said as I set my purse down on the counter. "After the disasters we used to come up with as kids..." I let out a soft laugh before it faded when I turned my gaze to Miles.

His lips were tipped up into a smile, but when he saw me notice, it disappeared. "Yeah. I've definitely learned a thing or two since you left."

I pinched my lips together. The last three words cutting deeper than I'd anticipated. *Since you left.* I swallowed hard and forced myself back to reality as I nodded. "I bet."

Silence fell between us. The awkwardness seemed to seep into my soul. The sad truth of it all was, there was no way we were ever going to go back to normal. Miles and I were destined to live our life in a strange sort of hellish limbo.

And I was not looking forward to it.

A scratchy noise filled the air. I looked around, and from the corner of my eye, I saw Miles unhook what looked like a baby monitor from his back pocket and stare down at it. I furrowed my brow.

"I should get back," he said, tucking the monitor away and turning to face me. "You have my number. Call me if you need anything."

Before I could ask him why he was carrying a baby monitor, he gave me a quick nod and pulled open the front door. Then he was gone. The silence of the cottage filled my ears as I took in a deep breath.

I was in no way ready to be here. But it didn't matter. I was on Harmony Island. I was staying mere feet from the inn that almost broke me.

I was going to have to face my past.

8

MILES

I DON'T KNOW why I foolishly thought that Shelby would join me for breakfast, but I woke up an hour early and spent the morning baking cinnamon rolls and a bacon quiche. I was busy pulling the cinnamon rolls from the oven when Miss Porter pulled open the back door and walked in.

"Wow," she said as she hung her purse on the hook.

She'd once been a kindergarten teacher at Harmony Primary school, but retired a few years ago. When Charlotte passed away, she made sure to let me know that she would be more than happy to watch Belle when I needed it since she lived just down the road and to the left.

With the reading of the will this afternoon, I'd asked her over to help get Belle ready and adjusted so that when I left, Belle wouldn't be upset.

I nodded in her direction as she wandered over to watch me drizzle icing on top of the rolls.

"Is this how you cook for your guests every morning?" she asked, swiping at a drip on the counter and slipping it into her mouth.

I wanted to say, no, this was a rarity. That I was so anxious to have Shelby sleeping next door that I'd gone and done something as stupid as baking an entire breakfast for a woman who would most likely never step foot in this place.

But I decided that was too much for a Monday morning with one of the town's well-known gossips. "Yep," I lied. "Every morning."

Her eyes widened as she continued to suck at the icing on her finger. Her grey hair was pulled back into a loose bun. Wispy curls framed her tanned, wrinkled face. "I'll have to tell my daughter she should stay here when she comes next month." She waved to the food. "She's a food blogger and would probably write a good review for you."

My stomach sank. As much as the inn could use the exposure, I wasn't sure I was ready to run at full capacity. Plus, I had Belle. I needed my life to remain simple. Even if Shelby's return threw a wrench in that plan.

I could only focus on so many things, and finding a firm footing was my top priority. Everything else could fall by the wayside. At least, for now.

"Thanks, but I think I've got enough guests for now," I

said as I took the mixing bowl and spatula to the sink to rinsed them off.

"You sure?" Miss Porter waved her hand in my direction as if batting away my comment. "I'll still tell her." Then her gaze got serious as she studied me. "She's single and you're..." Her voice trailed off, and I didn't have to look at her to know that she had a quizzical expression.

I sighed. Apparently, a single dad trying to run the local inn in a small town was very much in need of a wife.

There was nothing I wanted less than to confuse myself with the female part of the human race. I was struggling with the woman now sleeping in the cottage next door. The last thing I needed was to add another person on top of that.

"I'm good," I said over my shoulder as I sudsed up the bowl. "The only girl I need in my life right now is two and adorable in pigtails." I shot Miss Porter a smile.

She clicked her tongue in protest but didn't push it further. I thought I heard her mumble, "alone forever" and "I'm telling her anyway," but when I grabbed a nearby dishtowel, I found her moving around the kitchen, looking at pictures.

"It's truly a shame," she whispered as she leaned into a photograph of Charlotte standing under the peach trees on the far end of the property. Shelby was standing next to her with peach juice dripping down her chin and a large toothless grin.

I swallowed as I turned back to the sink. That picture

was taken a year before my dad married her mom. As kids, things were so much simpler. I would give anything to go back to that time. To see Shelby happy once more.

"What is?" I finally asked.

"She was such a happy woman back then. It's a shame she was taken from us." Mrs. Porter let out a sigh. "Or that her daughter was such a failure."

Anger rose up in my chest. There was so much to that story that the town didn't know. Which was surprising. Living in a small town, everyone knew everything. But Charlotte kept things close to her heart. It took a while before she even opened up to me about Emma.

"And that granddaughter."

From the corner of my eye, I saw Miss Porter tap on the glass.

"What was her name?"

I narrowed my eyes but forced my body to not turn around. I didn't want her to talk about Shelby, but I also didn't want to blow up at the woman either. I'd learned that in this small town it was best to let the busybodies say what they wanted to say and then move on.

But she was skating on very thin ice with steaming hot blades. If she didn't watch what she said...

I clenched my jaw and tucked the dishrag through the handle of the oven. "I'm going to check on Belle," I said as I passed by her. Removing myself from the situation seemed the best route.

Miss Porter parted her lips, but I didn't wait to hear

what she had to say. Instead, I just nodded and made my way through the back hallway to Belle's room.

Thankfully, she was awake, so I turned my attention to her. After getting her a pink dress from her closet—the grandmothers of Harmony were very generous after Tamara dropped Belle off and threw me a baby shower—I walked over to her crib. She was standing along the railing, grinning up at me.

Her hair was matted and stuck up in different directions, but I couldn't help but smile right back at her.

"Good morning, my princess," I said as I set her dress on the changing table next to her crib and scooped her up. I helicoptered her a few times before bringing her down and smashing a kiss into her soft cheek. She giggled and pushed against my chest, so she could look me in the eyes.

"Did you have a good night sleep?"

She babbled a few things as I laid her on the changing table and unzipped her pajamas. It didn't take long for me to change her and get her dressed. After I was done, I set her onto the ground, and she puttered around while I grabbed her brush. She only screamed a few times as I attempted to comb out the tangles and pull it all back into a ponytail.

That was as far as I went with her. It did make me sad that she didn't have a mother to do fun things with her hair. And even though I'd never admit it to anyone, I'd started watching YouTube videos at night to learn how to braid hair. There was no way I could ask anyone in town to help me.

That was a part of my life that I didn't want to circle around on the gossip train.

I opened Belle's door, and she followed me out of her room. I walked into the kitchen, half expecting Miss Porter to still be standing there, muttering under her breath as she looked at the pictures, but what I saw caused me to stop entirely.

Shelby was standing next to the door in pink satin pajamas with her arms wrapped around her chest and her eyes wide. Mrs. Porter was standing a few feet off, talking, but I could tell that Shelby wasn't listening. It was as if she were frozen to the spot.

I seemed to be the disruption she needed, because as soon as I entered the room, her gaze snapped to me. Her eyes looked desperate.

"We've all been wondering where you've been. After the funeral, you ducked out of town so fast, I swear I saw smoke coming off your feet," Miss Porter said, followed by a loud laugh.

I cringed as Shelby seemed to retreat further into herself. Whatever Shelby had been expecting when she walked into the kitchen in her pajamas, I was fairly certain, Miss Porter was not it.

"Hey," I said, stepping forward. I crossed the room and blocked Shelby from Miss Porter with my body. I wrapped my hands around her shoulders. Then I leaned in and whispered, "Trust me." It was hard to ignore the way her whole body tightened from my touch, but I understood her reaction, and I was here to help her through it.

"Let me show you something," I said as I started to guide Shelby toward the hall.

"Show her?" Miss Porter asked from behind me.

I nodded and glanced over my shoulder. "Keep an eye on Belle. I'll be right back," I said as I disappeared with Shelby.

She was tight as I led her down the hall and into my room. It felt strange, having her come in here, but I pushed that thought from my mind as I led her over to my bed and pressed gently down on her shoulders.

Thankfully, Shelby didn't fight me. She dropped her hands to rest on the bed and sat hunched forward.

"I'll get Miss Porter busy with Belle, serve breakfast, and then come check on you," I whispered, not wanting my voice to startle her.

Shelby nodded but didn't look up to meet my gaze.

I looked back only once as I quietly shut the door behind me. Once I was out in the hall, I clapped my hands together. The desire to get everything situated so I could get back to Shelby coursed through me.

I quickly made Belle some breakfast and then gave her a kiss on the cheek as I gathered the cinnamon rolls and pulled the quiche from the oven. I pushed through the swinging door to the dining room where one of the guests was already sitting at the table with a cup of hot coffee in front of him.

I gave him a quick nod as I set the food on the buffet. He grunted and moved over to the food. I offered him a quick, "Enjoy," before I pushed back into the kitchen. Miss Porter was singing "The Wheels on the Bus" to Belle as she giggled, showing all the eggs she'd stuffed in her mouth.

I told Miss Porter to take Belle out to the small playground area I'd built last year when she was finished. Miss Porter nodded but didn't stop singing.

With everything situated, I stood there, feeling the draw to go back to my room. But I also wanted to make sure Shelby had enough time to calm down. I didn't want to push her further than she wanted to go.

I busied myself with pouring a glass of ice water and grabbing a banana. I wasn't sure if Shelby had eaten anything, and I wanted to give her that option. Plus, it gave me an excuse to go back to my room.

I took a deep breath and headed down the hallway to stand in front of my door. I felt frozen as I stared at the handle. The truth was, I was being ridiculous, but I couldn't help it. My relationship with Shelby was so complicated, and yet, the last thing I wanted was for her to pack up and leave.

I'd finally got her back home, and I wanted to take this time to explain what had happened so many years ago.

Feeling like an idiot, I realized that it looked very

strange for me to be standing out in the hallway, crowding the door. I softly knocked a few times and waited. I wasn't sure what I was supposed to do when I didn't hear anything, so I slowly opened the door.

"Shelby?" I asked as I hovered in the doorway. If she didn't want me to come in, I wanted to make my retreat less awkward.

"You can come in," she said softly.

I nodded and pushed the door open all the way. Shelby had moved from my bed and was standing near the window, looking out. Her arms were crossed, and she looked so small. So broken.

I wasn't sure what to say or where to stand, so I lingered close to the door. "I brought you some water and a banana," I said wincing at the sound of my own idiotic words.

Shelby turned her head to me slightly and then focused back on the outside world. "Thanks."

I nodded and then stood there. Did she want me to bring it over to her? Did she want me to just stand here? What was I supposed to do?

We remained silent for what felt like an eternity before she sighed, turned, and walked over to me. When she was about a foot and a half away, she held out her hands. My heart pounded as she stood there with an expectant look on her face.

I quickly handed the items over, and she took a long sip of the water. Her skin was pale. I could see the soft splash of freckles across her nose that would always darken in the summertime. She was older now but still just as beautiful as she was when we were teens.

When I'd fallen in love with her.

Thankfully, she never knew how I felt—I was pretty certain she thought I hated her. Or at least, that all I wanted to do was torture her. But that couldn't be farther from the truth.

I was always going to love Shelby, no matter how much she hated me or wanted to push me away.

"Thanks," she whispered as she pulled the cup from her lips and held the base of the glass in her open palm. She didn't move to open the banana, and I contemplated asking if she needed help. But then I remembered the night she left. When she was packing her bags, with tears streaming down her face.

I'd wanted to help then, too. But she'd refused to speak to me.

I'd had so many words that I wanted to say to her. Reasons for why things happened the way they did with Clint. But she hadn't been interested. And I feared that, even after all of these years, she still wasn't interested.

"I heard scratching at the door."

Her words caught me off guard. I was pulled from my reverie and glanced down at her. "What?"

She took another drink of water. "At the front door of the cottage. I heard scratching."

I glanced over my shoulder in the direction of the cottage. "Scratching?"

She nodded, her eyes never leaving my face. "Yes. Do you know what it might be?"

I ran my hand through my hair and shook my head. "No."

"Guests haven't complained about it before?"

"No." Charlotte never mentioned it. But I decided to keep that tidbit to myself. I was fairly certain that if I revealed Charlotte used to live there, Shelby would leave.

She furrowed her brow. "Huh."

Silence. Again.

"I can look into it," I said as I shoved my hands into the front pockets of my jeans and shrugged.

She studied me and then nodded. "Okay."

"Okay."

She took another drink. "I should go get showered," she said as she gestured to her pajamas.

I tried not to let my gaze slip down to her legs, but I couldn't help it. If I'd thought she was beautiful and sexy back when she lived here, things had only changed for the better. She was shapely and smooth. The satin material clung to all the right places.

Heat pricked at my neck, and I cleared my throat, hoping it would clear my mind of these thoughts.

"Okay," I said as I stepped to the side, so she could walk through the door. She paused before nodding. Just as she passed me, I remembered the breakfast that I'd woken up so early to make.

"I made cinnamon rolls and a bacon quiche." The words tumbled out before I could stop them.

After a moment, she took in a deep breath and turned to study me. "Listen, Miles. I made a mistake coming into the inn in the first place. Coming to Harmony was already hard enough, and I'm fairly certain I'll break if I push myself anymore. I'm here for the will reading, and that's it." She offered me a weak smile.

I nodded—probably a bit too quick. "I get it. I just thought..." My voice trailed off as sadness peeked through the hard shell she had wrapped herself in. "I won't ask again," I said, my voice dropping an octave as the desire to protect her surged in my chest.

"It was a mistake," she whispered as she shifted the banana to the hand holding the water and pulled open the door.

I contemplated following her out but decided against it. It seemed like the thing she needed right now was freedom from me. Freedom from her past. Freedom from her memories.

No matter how much I wanted to confront her, to fix the broken things in our past, I wasn't going to put that pressure on her. I was going to let her heal.

Even if it meant I needed to wait in the shadows.

9

SHELBY

SWEET TEA &
SOUTHERN GENTLEMAN

POUNDING.

That was the only way I could describe my heart rate right now as I walked through the inn's kitchen and out the back door. I'd been such an idiot coming in here this morning. First, running into Miss Porter had been unexpected. Then, there was the rush of emotions that coursed through my body as I stared at all the familiar parts of my grandmother's kitchen that I'd forgotten.

Thankfully, Miles saved me from my frozen episode, but then I ended up in his room—which had been my grandmother's back when I lived with her. Even though he'd changed everything—one would have never guessed that a ninety-plus-year-old woman had once lived there—it didn't change the fact that it had been hers.

There were memories that I made there that I would never forget. No matter how much I might want to.

I didn't stop walking until I got through the cottage's door, and I collapsed on the couch in the small living room. After setting the water and banana onto the coffee table, I leaned forward until my chest was resting on my thighs and my chin was on my knees as my hands flopped to the floor.

I closed my eyes and took in a few deep breaths.

I was in shock, that was all. Eventually, it wouldn't hurt me as much to see my grandmother's house. It wouldn't hurt this much to walk down memory lane.

Eventually, I would be fixed...

I hoped.

A few minutes later, I straightened and made my way to my bedroom. What I needed in this moment was to take a hot shower and blast my favorites playlist while I half sang, half cried until I felt better.

Steam filled the bathroom as I belted out Whitney Houston's "*I will always love you.*" I squeezed the bottle of bodywash until a large dollop appeared on my loofah. The smell of sweet pea and jasmine filled the air as I scrubbed my body.

Once I was clean and much more emotionally stable, I shut the water off and wrapped a towel around my body. I swiped at the cloudy mirror, streaking water across the glass. My cheeks were pink, so I looked a little more alive, which was nice.

After brushing my teeth, I opened the bathroom door and headed out to dress. I picked a soft yellow sundress with tan sandals. Then I headed back into the bathroom to put on some makeup. I was most likely going to run into people I knew at the will reading. There was no way I was going to look like the walking dead when that happened.

My life may be a mess, but they didn't have to know. I ran a brush through my hair as I blow-dried it, and once I was done, I surveyed myself. I was definitely older, but I wasn't too bad. Not when I made an effort.

I was going to rock any encounter coming my way. I was determined to.

I grabbed my purse from the dresser and opened the bedroom door. My entire body froze when I saw Miles standing in my kitchen with a tinfoil wrapped plate and a strange look on his face.

He was wearing a white button-down shirt with his sleeves rolled. It was tucked into a pair of dress pants. His hair was styled in a way that made one question if he'd done something or if it was naturally that tousled.

My heart picked up speed as I took him in, but I quickly pushed that reaction aside. I was just startled by his sudden appearance. That was all.

"Is this going to be a habit?" I asked as I pulled the strap of my purse up onto my shoulder and made my way into the kitchen like his presence had no effect on me.

"You still sing in the shower?" His voice was quiet and held a mocking tone.

I stopped, heat pricking my cheeks. "How long have

you been here?" I asked as I made my way over to a kitchen cupboard and grabbed a glass.

"Since you were singing," he said, his words steeped in the smile playing on his lips.

I filled the cup up with water and then took a sip, appraising him over the rim of the glass. "Is this going to be habit?" I asked again.

His smile remained. He was obviously amused with himself. "What?"

"You breaking and entering."

He stopped smiling and glanced around. "What?"

I set the glass down. "I get that you have a key and we were once related, but this is my place and you promised me that you weren't going to bother me." I quirked an eyebrow as realization passed over his face.

He set the plate down and shoved his hands into his pockets. "Sorry," he murmured.

Guilt clung to my stomach, but I refused to give in. Whatever relationship he thought we had, he was reading the room wrong. I was here for the will reading—I was determined to keep Missy from ever owning this place. But reigniting a relationship with Miles wasn't in the cards for me.

"What's that?" I asked, nodding toward the plate.

He shrugged. "I thought you might want more than the banana and water from earlier." His gaze drifted to the coffee table where the glass from the inn and the banana sat untouched. "Or instead of them."

My stomach was in knots, and the last thing I wanted was to fill it with food. Especially when I wasn't sure what the afternoon had in store for me. "I'm not hungry," I said.

Miles glanced down at the plate and then back up to me. "Should I stick it in the fridge?" he asked.

"Sure."

After he set it next to the yogurt, he turned. "I also wanted to ask if you want to ride to Tom's office together. You know, save on gas."

I studied him. He appeared nonchalant, but I wondered if he really didn't care or if he was just trying to appear that way. I sighed as I leaned against the counter with my hip. "I guess," I said.

Truth was, I was tired, and the last thing I wanted to do was try to navigate the streets of Harmony. I had no idea where Tom's office was, and I wasn't really in the mood to figure it out. If Miles wanted to take the lead on this, I was willing to let him.

"Really?" he asked, his voice surprised as he raised his gaze to meet mine. There was a spark there that made me feel bad.

Things changed between Miles and me when Clint walked out and I lost the baby. I knew Miles had something to do with it, but he never came clean. It was hard not to be frustrated with him.

It took a few years, but I finally came to the conclusion that Clint had left because he wanted to. Our relationship had turned rocky, and Clint had become distant. Miles just gave him the excuse to leave when he did.

They were both to blame, but Clint was responsible for a bigger piece of that pie, even if Miles was currently taking the brunt of my frustration.

"Sure," I said with a nod.

His smile was back as he clapped his hands together. "All righty."

An awkward silence fell between us as we both stood there, trying not to look at the other person. Not sure what to do, I moved over to the front door and pulled it open. "Let's go then," I said as I passed through the doorway to the small porch outside.

That seemed to snap Miles out of his stupor, and he crossed the living room to join me. He shut the door behind him, and I locked it with my key. Then we walked side by side along the driveway to the small garage behind the inn. The same one that Clint first kissed me behind when we were sixteen.

I swallowed, a lump forming in my throat as I pushed those thoughts from my mind. I kept my gaze focused on the ground in front of me. I could do this. I could get through this. I was going to be okay.

I was going to survive.

Suddenly, two hands wrapped around my upper arms, and when I looked up, Miles's chest was inches from my face.

"Whoa," he said softly as he pressed against my arms to keep me from slamming into him.

I swallowed as I glanced up at him. "Sorry," I whispered.

His gaze was intense. "You okay?" he asked. It was so quiet, I almost wondered if it was just my imagination.

I pinched my lips together and nodded. "Yeah. Just lost in thought."

He studied me for a moment and then let me go. "Just keep your gaze up, okay? I might not be there to stop you from running into something that could really cause some damage."

Embarrassment coursed through me as I nodded and gave him a mini salute. "Yes, sir," I said before I felt like a complete idiot.

He hesitated then turned to pull open the passenger door for me. I didn't wait. I climbed into the car and slammed the door shut behind me. I used the time it took for Miles to round the hood to take a few deep breaths before he was behind the wheel and starting the engine.

We drove in silence to downtown Harmony. He parked, and I hopped out of his car before he could say anything. I was ready to get this over with and move on with my life.

I'd already put Harmony in the rearview mirror. Leave it to my grandmother to force me back down this road.

Thankfully, the wait to see Tom was short, and he invited

us into his office just a few moments after we'd arrived. He was an older man. Probably in his fifties. He was wearing a dark-blue, faded suit and his smile reminded me of the man who always played Santa at the church's Christmas festival.

He motioned toward the chairs in front of his desk as he shut the door behind him. I took a seat, and Miles followed a few feet behind me as if he were waiting to see which chair I would pick.

"Thanks for joining me," Tom said as he held his tie to his chest and sat behind his desk.

I'd picked the farthest chair. I crossed my legs as I turned my attention to Tom. Miles nodded as he sat, resting his elbow on his knee. "No problem," he said.

Tom's gaze found its way to me. "And you are Shelby?"

"Yes," I said, weaker than I liked. I cleared my throat and said, "Yes," more forcefully this time.

He smiled as he stood slightly, so he could reach across his desk. "Tom Holland."

I rose slightly to shake his hand.

"I moved to town after you left, but your grandmother talked about you so much that I feel like I know you."

There was so much weight to that sentence that all I could do was nod. I didn't have the strength to respond, so I remained silent.

Tom settled back in his seat, and his smile remained. He was in a good mood. It made me wonder how much my grandmother had really told him. What parts she shared and what parts she purposely left out.

"Thanks for joining me today. Having you both here will make this so much easier."

"Of course," Miles said as he straightened his back before slouching against his chair.

I'd known Miles long enough to know his physical signs. He was uncomfortable. I drew some comfort in that. He had always been so strong, so seeing him rattled made me feel calm and less alone.

Tom reached into a drawer and pulled out a stack of paper. "I've been going over your grandmother's will, and she wanted to leave the inn to the two of you."

I stopped. "Both of us?" I asked, wiggling my finger between Miles and me.

Tom cleared his throat and nodded. "Yes."

"Oh."

Miles glanced over at me before returning his attention to Tom. "But more of it goes to Shelby, right?" He leaned forward as if all he needed to do was glance down at the paper to confirm his words.

"No. It's fifty-fifty," Tom said as his gaze scanned the paperwork.

"It's fine," I said quickly. Gran saw Miles as her grandson. I couldn't be upset that she wanted to leave him half her belongings.

Tom glanced up at me from over his glasses. "I can read it again if you think I might have made a mistake."

I swallowed. "No. It's fine. We each get half the property. Perfect."

"Well, not quite."

My mind was swimming. "What does that mean?" I asked, my voice taking a hoarse tone.

"She did have a stipulation."

"Of course," I whispered.

Miles glanced over at me before returning his gaze to Tom. "Stipulation?"

Tom nodded. "In order for the inn to be sold, both parties need to be in agreement. And..." He hesitated as he flipped to a page with a sticky note. "...*both parties have lived at the residence for six months.*"

My heart completely stopped. I had an out-of-body moment as I stared at Tom. It was as if my body was held down by gravity, but my soul had risen up to stare down at me.

To pity me.

"Excuse me, what?" My voice was loud and squeaky, and it caused Miles to glance over at me once more.

"Yeah, what?" he asked.

Tom set the papers back down and shuffled them into place. "At the end of the six months, if you both don't agree with what to do with the house, then the house will go up for auction." He placed his hands on top of the papers and studied us, his gaze flicking from Miles to me.

Silence filled the air as we both tried to process what had been said.

"So, we both need to live at the inn for six months, and we both have to agree to selling the property?"

Tom nodded.

"And what happens if one of us wants to sell after the six months but the other one doesn't?"

My question must have startled Miles because he looked over at me as my words hung in the air.

Tom returned to the stack of paper to consult.

"You don't have to do this," Miles whispered, leaning across the divide between us.

I didn't acknowledge his words. As much as I didn't want to live at the inn for six months, I had nothing to go home to in New York except a strange sort of fake relationship. But I was pretty certain that Titan would understand my predicament. And if it meant that Missy wouldn't get the inn, I was willing to do just about anything.

"There is an option of one buying the other one out," Tom said, returning his gaze to the two of us.

"I'm never going to have that—" Miles started.

"We'll figure something out," I said as I pulled my purse up onto my lap and shot Tom a large and phony smile. I was ready to get this meeting over with. I now knew Gran's stipulations, and it didn't matter if I felt they were fair or not. They were what they were, and I was either going to go along with them or fight them.

Tom's smile moved to match mine. "Wonderful. This was easy," he said as he shuffled the papers once more until they lined up.

"Great." I stood. "If that's all, then I'll go," I said as I started toward the door.

"Wait. Don't you want to hear what else she left you?"

My hand was on the door handle, and freedom was mere moments away. "Nope," I said over my shoulder. "It can all go to Miles. As long as the inn is safe for now, that's all I care about."

I shut the door before either man could respond. I nodded toward Tom's receptionist and hurried out of the building. It wasn't until I was standing in the parking lot that I remembered I'd come with Miles.

I tipped my face toward the sky and closed my eyes, cursing my judgment. I didn't want Miles to find me before I had a minute to gather my thoughts, so I hurried down the side of the building and rounded the corner, where I almost ran into a woman standing outside of a store.

Her eyes were wide as I stopped myself mere inches from her.

"Whoa," she said as she held her hands up. Then she studied my face. "Are you okay?" she asked.

I peered behind her toward the small bookstore she was standing in front of. "Do you own this place?" I asked, my heart pounding in my ears.

She nodded. "I do."

I swallowed and gave her the best not creepy smile I could manage. "Wonderful." I glanced at the sign in the window that said *Coffee and Food Available*. "I am famished. Do you mind me coming in?"

She studied me and then nodded. "Sure. I just pulled some poppyseed muffins out of the oven."

My stomach growled. "That sounds amazing."

"Great."

She pulled open the door and a small bell chimed. "What's your name? I haven't seen you around here."

That was perfect. Someone who didn't know me or my past. This was just what I needed. "Shelby," I said with a smile.

She hesitated, her brow furrowing as if trying to recollect where she'd heard my name before. But then her expression softened as she extended her hand to guide me in. She gave me a smile. "It's nice to meet you, Shelby. This is The Shop Around the Corner, and I'm Abigail."

10

ABIGAIL

SWEET TEA &
SOUTHERN GENTLEMAN

I FOLLOWED behind Shelby as she walked into the bookstore. Her eyes were wild, and she looked as if, given the chance, she would sprint right down Main Street, never to be seen again. If I could help her calm down, I would.

Once we were inside, I gave her a small smile as I guided her to the back counter. The air in the bookstore smelled like lemon and sugar, and I caught Shelby's eyes widen as her gaze landed on the muffins I'd set on the cooling rack.

"They are amazing," I said as I grabbed a small saucer from the cupboard and set a muffin on top of it. I slid it across the white quartz counter as Shelby sat on the barstool.

She didn't say anything as she pulled the wrapper off and took a large bite of the top. Her eyes closed, and a soft moan escaped her lips. I laughed as I moved to the coffee pot. "Can I get you a drink to wash that down?"

Her eyes opened, and she nodded. "Do you have apple juice?"

I nodded and set the pot back down before I opened the fridge and grabbed a bottle of freshly processed apple juice. Mrs. Trumador supplied all the shops in town with freshly processed juices. Whatever she did made everything taste amazing.

I filled a glass and set it down in front of Shelby. Not wanting to stare at her while she ate, I leaned against the counter and slipped my phone from my back pocket. My heart raced as I glanced down at the screen to see if Anders had texted me.

Nothing.

Feeling like an idiot, I set my phone, screen down, on the counter and folded my arms. Of course, he didn't text me. Just because Fanny had seen him take my business card didn't mean that he was going to use it—even if I wanted him to.

He was just a construction worker here in Harmony. This place was a job, and I was just a pretty face for him to flirt with. Just because he'd picked my bookstore over anywhere else to get his coffee, didn't mean that he was my destiny.

I squeezed my eyes shut as I tried to force those thoughts to the back of my mind. I was being childish, and I needed to get my head on straight. Diving into someone else's problems seemed like the perfect distraction.

I opened my eyes and turned to focus on Shelby, who was almost done with the muffin. I quirked an eyebrow. "Did you skip breakfast?" I asked as I pulled open a drawer next to me and set a napkin down in front of her.

She picked it up and covered her lips. "I was a nervous wreck, so I didn't eat anything. Now I'm regretting that."

I tapped the counter with my fingertips. "Because of the will?"

She stopped and then glanced up at me. "You know about that?"

"It's a small town," I said with a shrug, hoping to cover the embarrassment I felt now that Shelby knew I was part of the gossip circle.

She sighed. "Yes. I know."

I studied her, wanting to ask her questions, but not wanting to be rude.

She fiddled with the last bit of her muffin as if she'd suddenly lost her appetite. "You can ask me," she said softly.

I swallowed, feeling like an idiot that this was our first meeting and I was standing here, gaping at her. "I'm sorry," I said as I straightened and grabbed a can of soda from the fridge. The sound of the tab breaking filled the air, and I took a sip. "I'm just distracted. Having you here is helping me keep my mind off my own thoughts."

Shelby studied me for a moment before she turned to survey the bookstore. "This is such a cute shop," she said.

I nodded. "I love it. I inherited it after my grandmother passed. It doesn't sell a lot of books, but stories are my life, so I knew I wanted a place for readers and coffee drinkers to feel comfortable." I set my soda down on the counter and then leaned forward on my elbows as I ran my gaze around the store with Shelby.

A sort of pride rose up in my chest as I took in the lines of bookshelves I dutifully stocked. I hated that the books didn't make much income; the food did. But if selling the food kept the lights on, I couldn't complain. I was truly living the dream.

"What's the problem?"

Shelby's question drew my attention over to her. "What?" I asked.

She waved toward me. "You said you needed a distraction. What's the problem?"

I drummed my fingers on the countertop as I studied her. Then I sighed and straightened. "Guy problems."

A smile played on her lips. "I should have guessed." She narrowed her eyes. "Want to share specifics? I could use a distraction myself." She sighed as she tucked her hair behind her ear.

I leaned back on the counter, folding my arms across my chest and dropping my gaze to my feet. "It's just hard, finding a guy in a small town."

Shelby's cheeks flushed as she studied the crumbs on

her plate. "I get that. Especially here in Harmony." She raised her gaze back up to me and gave me a weak smile. "If people are talking about me coming back, I can only guess that you know my complicated history here." She shrugged and then reached for her glass of apple juice.

"I know a little," I said.

She laughed. "Only a little? If Missy had her way, she'd share every sordid detail with anyone who would listen. She'd warn the whole world about how I'm no good and ruined her son." Shelby was staring at the countertop now. She let out a sigh, her shoulders rounding as she exhaled.

I wasn't sure what to say in response, so I just stayed quiet.

"Sorry," she whispered as she finished the apple juice and set the now empty glass down in front of her. "I have issues with this town, if you can't tell."

I gave her a soft smile. "I get it. I've run away, too."

She glanced up at me before picking up her napkin and wiping her fingers. "You have? What were you running from?"

Heat rushed across my skin. I didn't talk about Mom that much. Or think about her. And ever since Dad showed up in Harmony last year with Penny, I'd written my past off like a bad dream. We were attempting to make it work as a family, and even though we weren't perfect, we were trying.

At least, *I* was trying.

Sabrina was...surviving. But she was dealing with the disappearance of Trevor. As much as I wanted her to move on for Samuel's sake, I knew I couldn't push her further than she wanted to go.

"Parents," I said with a soft smile.

Shelby blew out her breath. "I hear that." She set her elbows down on the countertop and rested her chin in her hands. Her gaze softened as she stared off into the distance. "Does it get any easier?"

I shrugged. "Maybe? Time helps because we start to forget. But when we remember, that's when the pain shocks us back into consciousness. It's really not fair."

Shelby closed her eyes. "It's really not," she whispered.

Silence fell between us once more, but this time, it felt less awkward. We both knew what pain was like, and in a way, that pain was bonding us together. It was as if our souls were speaking to each other. There were no obligatory apologies for the pain we experienced in the past like we would get if we were speaking to someone who didn't know deep loss.

We were both aching from a past we could never go back and fix. It was a pain experienced only by a person who lost a part of their soul.

"Wow," she whispered as she glanced back over to me. "I did not mean to bring you down with me." She brushed some of the crumbs off the counter and into her hand.

I shrugged. "It's okay. I asked for a distraction, and you delivered," I said with a smile.

She snorted. "That I did." She brushed her hand off over her plate and smiled up at me. "You're like my bartender."

I grabbed the glass on the counter in front of her and set it in the sink. "I guess I kind of am."

Before she could say anything, the front door bell chimed, and we both looked over. Missy was talking on her phone as she stepped into the store, her gaze down-turned. Shelby whipped back around, a panicked look crossing her face. I didn't have to read her thoughts to know that she was begging me to help.

I nodded and waved for her to come around the counter. Shelby raced to my side, and I pressed her toward my office. She was safely inside with the door shut before Missy stepped up to the counter. She had finished her conversation and was looking around.

"I—er..." She bent backwards to peer down one of the book aisles. "Wasn't there..." She paused. "Was it just you here?" she asked as she pressed her finger down on the counter for emphasis.

I nodded and smiled—probably a bit too big. "Yep. Just me."

She furrowed her brow as she glanced around. Her gaze landed on Shelby's plate. "Whose is this?"

I leaned across the counter and pulled it toward me.

"Mine. I was eating it when you walked in." I pulled open the drawer where the garbage was hidden and dumped the crumbs. "I just hadn't cleaned up yet," I said with a smile as I set the plate in the sink.

"How's your morning going?" I asked as I grabbed the washcloth and began to clean the remaining crumbs from the counter.

Missy sighed, which I took as a good sign. She was going to drop the whole, "I thought someone was here with you," thing.

"Awful. I've been waiting to hear about the results of Charlotte's will reading, and I haven't heard anything." She set her purse down on the counter and tapped her chin as she stared at the menu board on the wall. "I need some chocolate and coffee," she said.

I nodded and got started making her non-fat, no whip, iced macchiato. We didn't speak while I worked, and after I set the coffee down on the counter, I grabbed her a triple chocolate chip cookie. I thought she was going to take her things and leave, but she slipped onto the barstool and unwrapped the cookie instead.

"I mean, how hard is it to just tell me if I can buy the place?" she asked, her mouth full of cookie.

I shrugged, wishing I had something more to do than just stand there and engage in this conversation. "I don't know," I murmured.

"It's not like Shelby wants to run the place." Missy

took a sip of her coffee and looked at me over the rim. "Did I tell you what she did to my Clint?"

I winced, wondering if Shelby could hear from the office. There was no way I wanted to have this conversation, but I didn't know how to get rid of Missy when she was determined to stick around.

"I don't—"

"She spread her legs for my son, got pregnant, and ruined his chances for a football scholarship, that's what she did." Missy's cheeks were red now as fire burned in her gaze. She was violently chewing on the bite of cookie she'd just slipped into her mouth.

"I'm sure—"

"And then for her to come back here like nothing happened and run that inn?" Missy shook her head as she took a long sip of her coffee. "This is my town. I'm the one who stuck around to pick up the pieces she left behind."

"Missy, I—"

"Just be grateful that you didn't know that girl." Her phone rang, cutting off her rant. She shoved the rest of her cookie into her mouth as she swiped her phone on and brought it to her cheek. "Hello?" she practically yelled through the food in her mouth. She wedged her phone against her shoulder as she grabbed her purse and coffee.

I didn't get so much as a cursory nod as she hurried out of the shop, and I collapsed against the counter once she disappeared around the corner of the building.

This was stressful for a Monday morning. I scrubbed my face with my hands and took in a deep breath. If I wanted a distraction from Anders, it was working. I glanced over my shoulder toward my office and winced. I really hoped that Shelby hadn't heard Missy, but I knew better than to believe that.

I was starting to understand a little bit more about this town and its ghosts, and I felt bad that Shelby was taking the brunt of it. I squared my shoulders and headed toward my office. I knocked softly before I turned the handle.

"Shelby?" I asked as I peered around the door.

She was sitting in my chair, staring at the wall in front of her. Her arms were wrapped around her chest, and she was completely still.

"Missy's gone," I said as I stepped inside.

She startled as she turned to face me. Her skin was pale, and she looked visibly shaken. "She is?"

I nodded. "It's safe."

Shelby nodded and stood. "Thanks for not telling her that I was hiding out back here."

I shrugged. "Of course. We've got to look out for each other."

Shelby's frown softly turned into a small smile. "Thanks. And I agree."

"Is there anything I can do to make you feel better?"

She shook her head. "I just need some fresh air and a walk." She took in a deep breath. "That'll help."

"Definitely." I wanted to offer to go with her. It probably wasn't best for her to be alone when she just went through that. But I had the shop, and Fanny didn't get here until four.

Shelby gave me one last smile before she pushed past me out into the store. I watched her as she gathered up her purse.

"Hey, here's my number," I said as I rounded the register and jotted it down. "Give me a call, and we can do something." I held out the paper and waited for her to take it.

She glanced at the paper before slipping it into her purse. "I'd like that."

"Great." In a small town like Harmony, it was hard to form new friendships. Most were formed when they were in diapers. By the time adulthood came, they were all well established.

Call me crazy, but the only person I had to talk to was Sabrina—and now Anders, hopefully—and that wasn't enough. I needed a friend in a bad way. If Shelby needed that too, then our relationship would be a win-win.

"Thanks for the food and the rescue," she said as she nodded back toward the food counter.

"Of course. Anytime you need me, I'll be here to listen."

She glanced outside through the glass door and sighed. "Thanks. I'm going to need that."

"So, you're sticking around Harmony, then?" I leaned

forward on my elbow, wanting to make sure that I caught every word she said.

Shelby glanced down at her purse and then back over at me. "I'm going to try." With that, she pressed on the door and headed out into the bright morning light.

With the shop now empty, I made my way back to the counter and started to clean up Missy's mess. My hands were plunged deep into the hot, soapy water when the front door opened once more.

"I'm back here," I called out.

Miles rounded the bookshelves and headed straight in my direction. "Have you seen a woman? She's about this high" —he held his hand up to his chest— "probably looked ticked off as all get out?"

"Shelby?"

His eyes widened. "She was here?"

I nodded. "She was here. She ate and left." I lifted my hand out of the hot water, so I could study my watch. "Probably about five minutes ago."

He cursed under his breath as he stared at the ground. I could see that his mind was whirling with thoughts. He glanced back up at me. "Did she say where she was going?"

I shook my head. "Nope. Just that she needed fresh air and sunshine."

He started to back away. "Thanks," he said.

Before I could even say, "You're welcome," he was gone. I turned my focus back on the dishes and sighed.

If I were looking for a distraction, my wish had been granted.

Having Shelby back in town was definitely shaking things up. Only time would tell if it was a good thing, or if I was going to regret ever getting involved with this decade-long situation.

11

MILES

SWEET TEA &
SOUTHERN GENTLEMAN

SHELBY WASN'T BACK YET. It was well into the afternoon, and she still hadn't resurfaced. I paced in the inn's front room, staring out the large picture windows and waiting for her to come walking up.

I'd thought about driving around Harmony looking for her but decided against it. Miss Porter needed to be back home, so her grandkids didn't come home to an empty house. When I got back, I'd made Belle lunch and put her down for a nap.

It was now two p.m., and I was stressed.

"I should have gone after you," I murmured. I walked up to the window closest to the wall full of books and leaned on the shelves as I surveyed the grounds.

Would Shelby be able to make her way back? Sure, she'd lived here her whole life. But it had been a while.

Would she recognize her hometown enough to find her way?

"Idiot," I said as I swore under my breath. I should have tried harder to find her. After she ran out of Tom's office, I had to stay behind to get the details. I'd figured she'd go to the car or sit outside to blow off some steam. I hadn't imagined she would just leave.

Gone.

The thought that maybe she was gone forever raced through my mind before I pushed it out. Shelby was suffering from PTSD when it came to Harmony, but she also hated Missy. There was no way she was just going to walk away and let Missy buy Harmony Inn. Shelby had too much pride.

"She'll come back," I said in a pathetic attempt to calm myself.

Belle's cooing came through the monitor clipped to my pocket, so I straightened and headed to her room. She had major bed head, so I took a second to comb out the snarls before setting her down and following after her as she waddled out of her room. I didn't have to lead her to the kitchen, she went there herself. After setting her up with a squeeze packet, I leaned on the counter in front of the back window and stared out at Charlotte's old cottage and Shelby's new home.

I wondered how Shelby would feel if I told her that her grandmother lived there before passing away, but then I shut that thought down.

I didn't want to live with the guilt—because I would crack if I lingered on it too long—and I already knew how she would react. She would pack her bags so fast and find another place to live.

No, if I wanted to keep Shelby close by, I would need to keep any mention of her grandmother to a minimum. Especially if we were going to be working together.

Six months. Tom's words echoed in my ears.

Six months. That was how long I was going to have to live with Shelby before we could sell. *If both parties wanted to sell.* I knew I didn't want to sell, but I was certain that Shelby did.

I also knew that I didn't have the money to buy Shelby out of the agreement. So right now, mine and Belle's future hung in the balance. And it sucked.

I blew out my breath as I scrubbed my face. Stress had built up in my shoulders, so I rolled them a few times to release the tension.

Belle giggled, and I glanced over at her. She was standing in front of her whiteboard with a blue dry-erase marker, scribbling. I crouched down next to her, wrapping my arm around her waist and planting a kiss on her cheek. "That's beautiful, squirt."

She turned and gave me a kiss before returning to her art.

Noise from outside caused me to stand. From the window, I could see Shelby talking to someone as she climbed out of a rideshare. She nodded and slammed the door, and it drove off. She lingered in her spot, raising a hand up to her eyes, so she could stare out at the cottage. Her shoulders had dropped, and I could see the pain in her expression.

I hated that she was broken. I wanted to pick up all the pieces. I wanted to fix her past. But I couldn't. Not right now. Not when she still hated me.

"Come on, princess," I said as I slipped my hands under her armpits and pulled her against my chest. I crossed the kitchen and opened the back door just as Shelby passed by.

She startled, whipping her gaze to meet mine. "Holy geez—" She brought her hand up to her heart and gripped her shirt. "You scared the crap out of me."

I winced and gave her an apologetic smile. "Sorry."

A confused expression passed over her face as her gaze landed on Belle. "Did you start a daycare at the inn?" she asked, dropping her gaze and heading toward the cottage. I didn't let that stop me. I was going to talk to her even if I didn't currently have shoes on.

I shifted Belle to the other side, using my forearm as a seat for her. "No," I said as I followed after Shelby.

"Do the guests know that you stole their kid?"

I glanced over at Belle, who had her head tipped back and was staring up at the trees above us. "I didn't steal her. This is my daughter."

Shelby stopped before she slowly turned to bring her gaze level with mine. "Your what?"

"You didn't know?"

She shook her head. "You're a dad?"

Pride swelled my chest. "Yes."

Shelby turned to study Belle before dropping her gaze, and we continued walking. "She looks nothing like you." Then she giggled. "Which is probably a good thing."

I scoffed and stared at Belle, who was currently sticking her tongue out at me. "What are you talking about? She looks just like me."

Shelby shook her head but didn't say anything right away. "So, you're married?"

I cleared my throat. "No."

She looked over at me. "What happened?"

Before I could answer, she held up her hand and shook her head. "Actually, don't tell me. I don't want to know. We have a business relationship, and that's it." She reached over and squeezed Belle's middle. My daughter squealed and pushed Shelby's hand away...before stretching back, beckoning Shelby to do it again.

I stared at her. We only had a business relationship? We were once friends. Once family. Once...

I cleared my throat as I dropped my gaze to the ground for a moment. It was obvious that I was the only one holding onto the past like it meant something. Shelby hadn't even known I had a daughter. In the three days she stayed here for the funeral, she hadn't bothered to ask what I was doing or what was happening in my life.

I'd spent so much time making sure she felt comfortable that I hadn't allowed myself to be upset that she hadn't asked me how I was coping. How things were going with me.

And now I knew why. I was a part of a past that she wanted nothing to do with. She was here to fulfill the terms of the will, and then she was leaving for good.

I was going to be the foolish man in the rearview mirror, pining after her.

"If that's what you want," I said, even though I wanted to say something completely different.

She met my gaze and nodded. "I think that's best, don't you?"

I sighed. This was not how I wanted this conversation to go. "So, what are your plans?"

She furrowed her brows. "What?"

"For the will. The stipulation. What's your plan? Are you just going to live in the cottage for six months? What about your job?"

Her expression stilled at my words. Suddenly, I realized there was something there. Something she wasn't telling me. Maybe her life in New York hadn't been perfect. Maybe...

Then her eyes widened and she whispered, "Titan."

I frowned. "What?"

She blinked a few times as if she were suddenly remembering something and then shook her head. "I'll have to call him."

"Is Titan your boyfriend?" The words came out fast and strong.

She studied me for a moment before turning her attention back to Belle. "I can help around outside. Like weeding and such."

I stared at her. Was she really not going to answer my question? Hating that I was now fixated on who Titan was, I pushed him from my mind as I glanced at the flower beds that wrapped around the inn and dotted the property. "Do you want me to fire Travis?"

"Travis?"

I nodded. "He's the landscaper I hired."

"Oh." She tapped her chin. "Well, no. I don't want you to fire him."

I wanted to ask if she could help at the inn. I flipped most rooms and did the cooking. "You could always help inside."

Her face paled, and I could see the word *no* float around in her gaze.

"It would be really helpful to me." I shifted Belle to my other arm. "Or if you watch Belle for me, I could get more done."

Shelby's eyes drifted to Belle. I wasn't sure, with the loss of her baby, if she was even willing to acknowledge other kids. But when her expression softened, I realized that I might have just discovered a winning plan.

"I guess I could do that." Then she wrapped one arm around her stomach. "And I could probably help with breakfast." Her gaze drifted back to me. "After all, I survived this morning in the kitchen."

I couldn't help it. A smile spread across my lips. "Really?"

She scoffed. "Don't look so excited. You may have gotten better at cooking, but I..." She shook her head. "All the years Gran tried to help me were wasted. I'm about as pathetic a cook as they come."

I shook my head as I laughed. "I doubt that."

"Just wait. I'll show you."

I didn't respond. Instead, I just stood there, smiling. I wanted to say that it was nice having her back. That I missed her more than I could ever express. But I didn't want to scare her, and I had a feeling any declaration like that would send her running for the hills.

"Dada," Belle said, breaking the silence as she slapped both of her hands on my cheeks and squeezed, causing my lips to puff out like a fish. Heat pricked my neck as I shifted her so she was facing out more. Shelby's smile was back, and I heard her soft laugh.

"I think Belle and I are going to get along together just fine." She held up her hand to Belle for a fist bump, and my daughter more than gleefully reciprocated.

"Great," I said as I brought Belle closer to me. "Traitor," I whispered, but made sure it was loud enough for Shelby to hear.

"Excuse me?" A soft, feminine voice sounded from behind me.

I turned around at the same time Shelby looked up, and my eyes widened. "Laura?"

Laura was wearing a white dress with stilettos that were digging into the grass as she walked toward us. "I'm so sorry. I waited at the desk, but no one came." Her gaze drifted to Shelby before coming back to me. "I even rang the bell."

From the corner of my eye, I saw Shelby start to back away. Not wanting her to misunderstand my relationship with Laura, I nodded toward Shelby's retreating frame.

"Laura, this is Shelby. Shelby this is Laura. My friend from Godwin's."

Shelby raised her eyebrows. "You have a friend from the grocery store?"

I could feel Laura's gaze on me before she shifted her focus to Shelby and extended her hand. "It's so nice to meet you," she said.

They shook, and Shelby pulled her hand away quickly.

"It's nice to meet you, too," she said as she reached out to pinch Belle's tummy once more. "I should go," she said as she gave a small wave and headed toward the cottage.

The air around Laura and I fell quiet. The only sounds pricking my ears were the wind rustling the trees and Belle's soft breathing. Knowing that I might as well face Laura head-on, I plastered on a smile. "What did you need from me?" I asked as I started walking across the yard to the back door of the inn that led into the kitchen.

"Well, you kind of left things open-ended when we saw each other last. I thought I'd come visit and see what this place is all about." Her voice softened. "And why people love it so much." When I glanced over my shoulder at her, I took note of the way her gaze was penetrating mine.

And I knew. I knew in that look. In the way she chewed her bottom lip. This wasn't some fact-finding mission. She was here to see me.

She wanted *me*.

My cheeks burned at that thought. I felt stupid for inviting this. I should have shut this down at the store. I wasn't in the headspace or heart-space to tackle a new relationship. I had Belle, and I was trying to wrangle Shelby.

Add in the inn, and I was all booked up.

"It's not much," I said as I pulled open the door and stepped inside. Laura didn't wait on the stoop or ask if she could come in. She just followed after me. Once inside, I set down Belle, who waddled over to her toys in the far corner and pulled them out.

I shoved my hands into my front pocket and glanced around. "Can I get you a glass of water?"

"Tea would be nice," she said as she crossed the room and sat at the small table I'd set up in the corner for Belle and me to eat at when the inn was packed. She situated herself on the small chair, crossing her legs and adjusting her skirt so it hit her knee perfectly.

I swallowed as I moved to the cupboard. I wasn't blind

to the female form. Sure, it had been a while since I'd been with a woman. But my last mistake had led to Belle. And even though I adored my daughter, I was going to make sure I didn't mess up again. One kid was enough to take care of by myself. It wouldn't be fair to add in another.

And even being perfectly safe could still lead to whoopsies.

I was whoopsied out.

"Tea," I repeated as I set the glass down and opened the fridge. I poured the amber liquid into the glass and then crossed the room to hand it to her.

She took a small sip and set the glass down on the table. "So, who is Shelby? Does she work here?"

Laura's question caught me off guard. I inhaled sharply, causing my spit to fling to the back of my throat. I coughed a few times, whacking my chest as I did it. "Shelby?" I finally wheezed as I attempted to move on from my embarrassment.

Laura offered me her tea, but I shook my head. She took a sip, appraising me as she did. "The woman you were talking to outside."

I glanced toward the back window and then nodded. "Her grandmother owned the inn. She's here to settle the estate."

Laura was still watching me as she finished her drink and set her glass down. "Did you two ever date?"

Wow. She shot straight from the hip. What an easy question to answer but with a loaded history behind it.

"No," I said, placing my hand on the table so I could drum my fingers. "We didn't date."

Now, if Laura had asked if I'd ever liked Shelby, that would be a whole other answer entirely. I not only liked Shelby; I'd fallen in love with her in high school. There hadn't been anything I wanted more than to be with her.

But she didn't want me. She'd never picked me.

Despite the fact that I was desperate to move on, my heart wasn't so easily convinced. I was left in this sort of limbo hell. I was desperate to get out, but I couldn't quite shake the shackles I felt whenever I was around her.

In short, I was miserable.

Laura took in a deep breath. "That's good to know. I'd hate to get involved with a guy when he was living so close to a woman he once dated." She turned to smile at me, the tone of her voice turning light as she smiled. "So, what does a girl have to do around here to get you to ask her out on a date?"

I parted my lips, but before I could speak, the back door opened, and Shelby was standing there with an empty plate in her hand and an innocent look on her face.

"I'm not interrupting, am I?"

12

SHELBY

SWEET TEA &
SOUTHERN GENTLEMAN

WHY DID I CARE?

I shouldn't care.

It was stupid of me to even entertain the thought.

I paced in my kitchen, trying hard not to let my gaze drift to the window that faced the back of the inn. I was trying hard not to stare at Miles and Laura as they turned and headed inside. And I was trying hard not to wonder what the two of them were saying to each other that had them looking so engrossed.

I was failing miserably.

My body shook as I finally stopped pacing and collapsed on the kitchen chair. It had been an emotionally draining day. First, with seeing Miss Porter when I walked into the inn. Then, the will reading. Then, my extremely long walk around Harmony Island. Then, finding out about Miles's daughter. And now this.

No wonder my muscles felt like a pile of goo. I'd been running at full steam, and I hadn't had a moment to take a deep breath and think.

I rested my forearm on the table and pushed the chair out far enough so that I could lay my forehead down on my arm. I closed my eyes, reveling in the darkness, and took in a few deep breaths.

What did it matter if Miles was talking to a girl? He had every right to do so. After all, I had a life outside of Harmony and our weird family history; it was only right for him to have the same.

My stomach growled, and I groaned as I grabbed at my middle. The only thing I'd had to eat was the muffin, and it was no longer satisfying me. I was certain I burned about three thousand calories during my walk, so I was famished.

I pushed away from the table, eager to distract myself. I padded over to the fridge and pulled open the door. One quick scan and I picked up the plate that Miles had brought over for me this morning. Based on the smells that had wafted around the kitchen, it was going to be delicious—even heated up.

I pulled off the tinfoil and stuck it in the microwave. It whirred to life, and I could see the plate spinning inside. I leaned down in front of the door and let my mind wander.

How long had Miles known Laura? Did he do this on the regular? Have single women over to the inn to "show them around?" What about Belle? What did he do with her?

And who was Belle's mother? Did I know her?

Where was she?

The microwave rang before my mind became an even more tangled mess. I blinked a few times and then straightened and pulled on the handle. The smell of bacon and cinnamon filled my nose, forcing out all my questions and leaving me with only one thought. Food.

I grabbed a fork from the drawer as I walked by and settled down on at the table. Before I even realized it, my plate was empty and my stomach was full.

I leaned back, licking the remaining frosting from my fork before setting it on my plate. With my hunger in check, my thoughts returned to Miles and Laura.

Was she still there?

I peeked over my shoulder and then sighed. I knew I shouldn't care that Miles had a girl over. After all, it was none of my business. But I also knew that I wouldn't sleep tonight if I didn't find out.

I didn't want to admit it, but I was jealous that Miles seemed so happy. He had a baby. He had women in his life. And here I was, trapped in my hometown by my grandmother and with a fake boyfriend I still had to reach out to.

It wasn't fair.

Why did he get to move on? After all, if it wasn't for him...

It didn't help dredging up the past. It only broke me

even more. I couldn't change what happened. Even if I wanted to.

I blew out my breath, determination pumping through my veins. If I was going to be miserable, so was Miles. He was the reason I was in this much pain, and he wasn't going to get off this easily.

I quickly washed the plate and dried it before tucking it under my arm. I took in a few deep breaths as I slipped on my shoes. The walk to the inn took less time than I'd anticipated, and as my feet hit the wood steps leading to the back door, I suddenly wanted to split.

No amount of frustration was worth the flashbacks I knew were coming if I set foot in the inn. But my body acted on its own, and suddenly my hand was on the door handle and I was turning it.

I could hear Miles and Laura talking before I could see them. But as I pushed further into the kitchen, I forced a smile as both turned to look at me. I slipped the plate out from underneath my arm and held it up.

"I'm not interrupting, am I?" I asked innocently as I made my way further inside before Miles could try to stop me.

Miles was off his chair before I made it to the counter. He took the plate from me and moved to set it in the sink. "Nope. Laura was just leaving."

I glanced over at Laura, whose eyes were wide. "I was?" she asked.

Realizing that I'd been wrong all along—this wasn't a

welcome interaction—my game plan changed. "She was?" I asked as I leaned in toward Miles.

He stiffened before glancing down at me. "Yep. I have rooms to tend to."

I frowned when I saw Laura wring her hands. She wanted to stay. She so obviously wanted to stay. But Miles? He wanted her gone.

This just got interesting.

"Where are you from, Laura?" I asked as I rested my hands on the counter next to me and pulled myself up onto it.

She flicked her gaze from me to Miles before she settled back on me. "Louisiana. I'm here visiting my aunt, Betty Lou Thompson."

I swallowed at the mention of Miss Thompson. She owned the antique shop in town, and there was a time or two that Clint had used me as a distraction so he could swipe her antique pipes.

"Oh," I said before I shook those thoughts from my mind and focused on the present. If Laura was just visiting, I doubted she knew who I was.

"And how long are you in town for?"

Miles turned to stare at me as if to say, "*Knock it off*," but I just shrugged off his look.

Laura fiddled with her purse. "A few weeks..." Then her gaze migrated to Miles, who was washing my plate over and over as if desperate to keep himself distracted.

"Unless..." she whispered, clearly hoping Miles would pipe up and ask her to stay.

"Well, Miles should take you out sometime. After all, he's lived in town a long time. And being part owner of the inn, he has the inside scoop on where the hidden gems are." I patted his shoulder. He stiffened before he turned around to glare at me.

"What are you doing?" he whispered as he leaned in so close that he was only inches from me.

Suddenly, a wave of heat flooded over me, startling me into silence. I blinked a few times, confused at what that reaction was. Thankfully, he'd straightened before I had time to dwell on it, and I brought myself back down to the present.

"It's the neighborly thing to do." The words came out weaker this time. This game was suddenly not as interesting as it had been.

He glared at me. "Don't you have somewhere else to be?"

"I'd really like that."

We both jumped and turned to see Laura standing next to us. Realizing that I'd forgotten she was there, I jumped down from the counter and waved my hand in her direction.

"She'd really like that," I parroted.

A small hand tugged on my dress. I glanced down to see Belle reach her chubby hands up. Out of instinct, I picked her up and set her on my hip. "I can babysit this

THE INN ON HARMONY ISLAND   147

little tyke. I bet it's been a long time since you've had a break."

My voice softened as I turned to look at Miles. He'd abandoned the dish in the sink and had turned to face us. His expression was stony, but there was a softness in his gaze as he stared at me and Belle. Not sure what to do, I brought Belle's cheek to mine and gave him a smile.

"She and I will do great." I waved my hand between the two of them. "Go. Have fun."

"I'm free Wednesday night," Laura piped up as if she didn't want to give him another chance to say no.

Miles glanced over at her before sighing. "You sure you want to go out with me? Ever since she came around" —he waved at Belle— "I'm not much of a partier." He sighed. "I'm in bed by seven most nights."

Laura laughed. "I'm fine with whatever you want to do." Then she dropped her gaze before slowly bringing it up, raking it over his body until she got to his face. "I love a man who would do anything for his daughter."

Miles eyes widened, and suddenly I felt very uncomfortable. It was fun when I was the one doing the prodding. But the situation had taken a completely different turn.

"Well, it's settled then," I said as I set Belle back down onto the floor. "I'll watch Belle, and you'll entertain Laura until seven." I grinned at the two of them. "It's a win-win."

Miles looked confused as if he'd just gotten whiplash.

He glanced from me over to Laura before shrugging. "I'm game if you are."

Her smile made me want to barf, but I clapped my hands, startling her. "Wonderful. I'm glad I came over to help out."

Laura giggled. "Me too." Then she sighed. "I should get back. Betty Lou will have a conniption if I'm gone while she's trying to close the store." Her gaze lingered on Miles. "I'm excited for our date."

Miles nodded. "I'll text you?"

"Perfect." She gave him one last long stare—as if she were afraid he would dissolve into thin air—then grabbed her purse, made her way to the back door, and disappeared outside.

When the sound of the door latching filled the air, Miles turned back around, resting his hands on either side of the sink. I turned too, so I could watch him. He was quiet as he stared outside.

"What are you trying to do?" he asked.

I frowned. "What do you mean?"

He growled before turning to look at me. "I'm not interested in dating anyone." He pushed off the counter and scrubbed his face. "I have too much going on in my life to bring someone else into it."

I sighed as I folded my arms. "It's one night. You'll be fine."

He tipped his face toward the ceiling and paused before bringing it back, so he could glower at me. "Stop."

His word cut through me, causing me to step back. There was a bite to his tone that I'd never heard before.

"Stop what?"

Anger flashed in his gaze. "Stop acting like you know me."

I scoffed. "What are you talking about? I do know you."

He shook his head. "No, you don't. You know the old Miles. Things have changed." His voice tightened as if emotions had lodged themselves there. "I'm not the same man I was before."

There was a depth to his gaze that shocked me. I took another step back as I appraised him. He wasn't wrong. Things had changed. He wasn't the lanky boy I knew as a kid or the tall young man I knew in high school. He'd filled out. I could tell from the way his t-shirt hugged his chest that he had muscles for days. His shoulders were broad, and his biceps caused the sleeves of his shirt to strain.

My cheeks heated as I dropped my gaze to the floor and stared hard at the spot in front of my feet. What was I doing? What was I thinking? Had I gone crazy?

Probably.

"I'm sorry," Miles muttered, drawing my attention back up.

"About what?"

He sighed as he leaned back, bringing his feet in front of him and folding his arms across his chest. "I'm just not ready for a relationship."

I fiddled with my dress, needing to think about something other than how much Miles had changed. "It's a date, Miles. Not a lifetime."

He peered over at me, his gaze dark. "I don't date like that anymore."

I swallowed. He was a man who knew what he wanted. And I? I was a fired, floundering, broken woman.

I envied him.

"Dating like that got me Belle. I love my daughter, but she's growing up without a mother. I couldn't do that..." His voice broke as he turned to set his hands on either side of the sink again before dipping his head forward and taking in a deep breath.

"I'm sorry," I whispered. I really hadn't meant to cause him this much stress.

He shook his head. "It's fine. I just never figured you for a matchmaker. You caught me off guard." He tipped his face toward me and gave me a small smile.

I found myself smiling. "It's that bad?"

He chuckled. "There's Miss Patty and her dog walker. Miss Trish and her second cousin's step-niece..." He continued, tapping each finger on the counter as he listed them off.

I raised my eyebrows. "So basically, the entire town is trying to marry you off?"

He nodded. "Everyone but Charlotte. She left me alone in the romance department." A sad expression passed over his face that I could only imagine matched mine.

But I knew his was for different reasons. Whenever I heard her name, my chest filled with pain. But I could only assume that when Miles talked about her, he genuinely missed her.

What might that be like?

I cleared my throat, suddenly feeling as if the walls of the inn were closing in on me.

I needed to get out of here.

"Well, I'm sure you will survive when you choose to go out with Laura," I said as I headed to the back door.

Miles straightened and turned. He looked confused as I reached out and turned the door handle. "Okay," he said as I stepped out onto the deck.

I bounded down the stairs and hurried into the cottage. Once inside, I leaned against the door and took a deep breath.

That whole situation had been so strange. I went from feeling devious, to sympathetic, to pain. My whole body felt as if it had been run ragged and left out to dry.

I pushed off the door and headed to the bathroom. I was going to take a hot bath and crawl into bed, where I'd watch chick flicks until I passed out.

I was going to forget everything about this day and wake up tomorrow anew.

It was the only way I was going to survive living here. Forgetting the past and just focusing on the present.

The future? Well, that was future Shelby's problem.

13

ABIGAIL

SWEET TEA &
SOUTHERN GENTLEMAN

SAMUEL WAS CRYING.

I rolled onto my side and groaned as I glanced over at my clock.

4 a.m.

Sighing, I grabbed the edge of my comforter and pulled it off my body as I slid my legs down the side of the mattress and fumbled to find my slippers. I pulled them on as I hopped to my door and down the hallway.

Samuel's crying grew louder as I neared his room. I pushed open the door and hurried to the side of his crib.

"Hey, hey," I whispered, reaching down and picking him up. Even though there was only a night-light in his room, I could see his beet-red face as he screamed. I brought him up to my shoulder and shushed as I bounced him up and down, then headed into the kitchen and opened the cupboard where his formula was.

"I know, I know," I sang as I fought off a yawn.

Once the bottle was made, I headed into the living room and settled down on the rocker. His crying instantly stopped as he nursed the bottle. I leaned my head back and sighed, closing my eyes as I used the tip of my big toe to push the rocker back and forth.

This wasn't the first time Sabrina had slept through his screams. I glanced over at her room. The door was shut, and there wasn't a hint of her waking up.

I closed my eyes once more. I knew she was tired, but what if I wasn't here? Would she just sleep through his cries?

Samuel shifted, causing the nipple to slip out of his mouth, which resulted in a large wail, but I managed to slip it back in quick enough that he calmed right down.

"Poor baby," I whispered as I closed my eyes and continued to rock.

Somehow, I managed to put him to bed and crawl back under my comforter. When I woke the next morning, I half expected to find myself sleeping in the rocker.

I yawned, feeling the effects of waking up before the sun, and stretched out on my bed. It took some convincing, but I finally slipped out of bed and padded over to my bathroom, where I showered.

Once I was dressed and ready to go, I pulled open my bedroom door to find the kitchen light on. Sabrina was sitting at the counter when I walked in, looking tired. She had a mug of coffee in front of her, and she was staring off into the distance.

"Sleep okay?" I asked as I made my way to the coffee machine and poured myself a mug.

She yawned and shook her head. "Not really."

I furrowed my brow. Then why didn't she get up with Samuel?

"Did you not hear Samuel crying last night?" I asked as I sipped my coffee, welcoming the warm liquid and praying its effects would be swift. I needed a pick-me-up.

She frowned. "No."

I set down my coffee and grabbed a banana from the counter. "It was, like, 4 a.m. and he was screaming." I took a bite. "Loud."

Her frown deepened. "I'm just really tired. I guess I missed it."

The bite in her tone felt like a slap in the face, and out of instinct, I swallowed my half-chewed bite of banana. I could feel it as it slid all the way down. "I didn't mean—"

"I'm going to shower before you go," she said as she slid off the barstool and made her way into the hall bathroom.

I blinked a few times, not sure what that had been. My gaze lingered on the bathroom door. Was she mad at me? I figured she'd want to know that she'd missed her son crying in the middle of the night. Maybe if she knew, she would be more apt to wake up.

I finished my banana and threw away the peel, wiping

my hands on the nearby dish towel. Ever since Samuel was born, it felt like she was pulling away from me. I hated it. I missed my sister. She was in this dark hole, and I wasn't sure I would ever get her back.

I sighed as I pushed my worries about Sabrina from my mind. It was probably all in my head, and if I pushed her too hard, she'd just disappear more. If I needed to take care of Samuel when I was around to lighten her mood, I would.

It was the least I could do.

When I went into his room, he was up and cooing at the mobile that Dad had bought him when he was born. It had stuffed seashells and sea creatures, and Samuel loved it.

When I picked him up, I realized he'd had a blowout, so I cleaned him up, dressing him in a white-and-black striped onesie. "You look like a robber," I said as I picked him up and brought him to my shoulder.

He cooed as I made my way into the kitchen to get a bottle started. By the time Samuel was done eating, Sabrina emerged from the bathroom. She was wrapped in a satin robe and disappeared into her room without saying anything.

I glanced down at my watch and sighed. If I didn't leave now, I was going to be late opening the store. If I was late, there was a chance that I was going to miss seeing Anders.

Even though I'd forced myself not to think about him,

I couldn't help myself. He intrigued me, and I was interested in seeing where things could go with him.

Thankfully, Sabrina pulled open her bedroom door and headed out into the living room five minutes later. I'd just set Samuel in his swing, so I hurried to grab my purse and slip the strap over my shoulder.

"I gotta go," I said as I pulled out my keys.

Sabrina nodded as she headed over to the couch and grabbed the remote. She settled down without so much as one look in Samuel's direction. I paused, glancing between them before pushing away the worry that was nagging at the back of my mind. Then I twisted the door handle and slipped outside.

I was just being paranoid, that was all. Sure, Sabrina seemed a little distant lately, but she was tired.

And so was I.

I climbed into my car, and before I knew it, I was pulling into my parking spot behind the bookstore. Miss Smitherson was taking out her garbage and I waved to her, but she just ducked her gaze, tightened her sweater around her chest, and hurried back into her store.

I sighed as I grabbed my purse and a few of the packages of books that I'd put in my car last night. I'd need to unload the rest of the boxes once I unlocked the back door.

After dropping off the first load of boxes in the backroom and setting my purse down in the office, I walked back out to my car...and froze.

A man dressed in black, with his dark hair draped over

his face, was standing next to my trunk, looking inside. My heart felt like it was going to pound out of my chest. I squeaked, and he must have heard because he whipped around to stare at me.

His bright blue eyes startled me as his gaze met mine. His jaw clenched and his brows drew together in a tight frown.

"I don't have any money," I whispered.

He looked me up and down before his frown deepened and he turned back to my trunk. He started shifting boxes around.

"It's just books," I said, a little too loud, as I stupidly stepped forward. I didn't realize I'd approached him, until I was grabbing onto his forearm. "Please, they are just books. They aren't worth much. Believe me. I don't make much money selling them."

He stopped moving and turned to stare at my hands on his arm. Realizing that it was probably a mistake to grab onto a man who was most likely going to kill me, I dropped my hands and took a step back.

"Sorry," I murmured. When he glanced up at me, I winced.

He stared at me for a moment before he turned back to my trunk. "I don't want your books," he mumbled as he continued moving boxes.

"There's no money back there," I whispered. I drove a basic car and wore basic clothes. There was nothing about my appearance or life that would make anyone think I was wealthy.

"I don't want your money," he muttered before he sighed. "There you are."

"What?" I asked as I shifted to peer into my trunk to see what he was looking for.

Tucked in his rather large hand was a small chipmunk. It was chirping as the man covered it with his other hand and straightened. It wasn't until he was standing that I realized just how close I was to him. He was startled as well, and for the first time, I saw an expression on his face that wasn't a scowl.

I stood there like a frozen idiot before I tucked my hair behind my ear and stepped back. "H-how did he get there?"

The man blinked a few times as if to snap himself out of a stupor. His scowl returned as he leaned down and let the chipmunk go. It raced away, ducking under the fence that lined the alleyway.

"There was a hawk eyeing him, and he ran inside," the man said as he dipped his face forward so his hair draped over his forehead once more.

"Oh..." I stood there with my lips still forming an *o* as he turned and started heading down the alleyway.

Confused why he was leaving so soon, I hurried after him. "I'm so sorry I yelled at you," I said as I attempted to match his stride.

He didn't stop or turn to acknowledge me.

"I just thought you were going to rob me. You know, because of what you're wearing." I motioned toward his clothes as if that was all the explanation needed.

He stopped, and it startled me so much that I almost tripped over my feet.

"So, you're shallow."

It took me a second to gather my bearings. But when I did, his meaning was not lost on me. "I'm not shallow."

He furrowed his brow. "But you just said you judged me on my clothes." Then his expression turned into a smile. "You're a liar."

"I'm not...I mean..." Words were flowing through my mind, but nothing was coming out.

He let out a short laugh and turned to start walking again.

"Hang on," I said, thankfully able to put that sentence together as I reached out and grabbed his arm.

Once again, his gaze dropped to my hand, and I quickly pulled it away. Why did I keep touching this stranger? I tucked my hands into my pant pockets just to make sure I didn't do it again.

He turned to face me, folding his arms across his chest and quirking the only eyebrow I could see behind his curtain of hair.

I took in a deep breath as I tried to process what had transpired over the last few minutes. "Listen, I just wanted to say thank you for getting the chipmunk out of my trunk." I glanced up at him with what felt like a strained smile.

"And you thought the best way to do that was by insulting my clothes?"

My lips were open, but no words were coming out. Instead, they were moving up and down like I was a fish on land, desperate for air. "I mean..." I scoffed and waved at him once more.

He raised his eyebrows like he needed me to spell it out. I sighed, my cheeks heating. I was already in this deep, I might as well keep digging. "When a single woman comes out of her store to find a large man, dressed in black, rifling through her trunk, the only conclusion she can come to is that you're there to kidnap her and to do all sorts of unmentionable things to her."

He stared at me as if he were processing my words. Then he scoffed, scrubbed his face, and muttered something that sounded like "I don't have time for this," before he turned his focus back to me. "Listen, lady—"

"Abigail."

He paused as he met my gaze and then continued. "Abigail. Doing 'unmentionable things' never entered my mind. And I didn't know that you were a lady, much less single. I was out for a walk and saw a chipmunk scurry into an open trunk." He brushed his hands together. "And now that I know you, I realize that no man would be crazy enough to kidnap you." He held my gaze for a second before he turned and walked away.

My brain didn't have time to process what he'd said, much less come up with a quippy retort. So, I just stood there in the alleyway, watching him walk away, until he turned the corner and disappeared.

"I'll have you know a lot of men want to kidnap me," I shouted, the words spilling out of my mouth before I could stop myself.

Mr. Harrison had just stepped out of his shop to toss a black bag of garbage into the community dumpster, and witnessed my word vomit. He quirked an eyebrow, and I wanted the ground to open up and swallow me whole.

I pinched my lips shut, crossed my arms, and tucked my hands under my armpits as I hurried back to close my trunk. There was no way I was unloading the rest of the boxes now. I'd tackle that later.

Once inside my shop, I locked the back door and then leaned against the wall and closed my eyes. I kept my lips shut and screamed as loud as I could.

Who was that man? Why had I never seen him here? And why was he such a jerk?

I pounded my fist on my forehead as I pushed off the wall.

What was that? Why had all of my mental processing abilities failed me? I must have sounded like an idiot, talking to him. No wonder he'd smiled at me. The things I'd said? I winced.

They were pathetic.

I was still writhing over our interaction when I pulled

a tray of blueberry muffins from the oven. I set them on the counter and went to unlock the front door, turning the closed sign to open at the same time.

I was muttering under my breath all the things I wished I'd said, and I didn't notice the door open until Anders was standing in front of the counter with a large smile.

"Morning," he said.

My heart stopped. Which was quite a contrast because it was pounding from frustration a few seconds ago.

"Anders," I stammered.

He studied me, his expression faltering as if he was worried that he wasn't supposed to be in the store. I blinked a few times, clearing my mind of the mystery man from earlier and turned my full focus on the man that made my entire body feel light as air.

"The door was open, so I thought I could come in," he said as he pushed his hand through his hair. His dark blonde hair was more styled today, and I wondered for a moment if he'd done that for me...and my heart melted.

"Was that okay?" he asked, breaking me from my thoughts.

"Hm?" I asked, not recalling what he'd just said.

He paused and then smiled, showing each and every one of his perfect teeth. "Me coming in here." He flicked his finger from his chest to the floor. "Was that okay?"

I glanced to the front door, not remembering if I'd

actually opened the store. With the closed sign facing me, I nodded. "Of course."

He took a step closer to the counter. "Good."

A heated silence fell between us, and his gaze lingered on my face. "You look amazing this morning," he said.

Heat burned my cheeks, and I couldn't fight the smile that spread across my lips. "You look good too."

He quirked an eyebrow. "Really?"

I nodded.

He pumped a fist in the air. "I showered today." Then he leaned forward and winked. "Just for you."

It was cheesy, but I was okay with cheesy. After all, it had been so long since a man had talked to me much less flirted with me. The fact that Anders had shown up after my embarrassing performance the other day, well, I was going to enjoy every corny pickup line he had.

"Can I get you a drink?" I asked.

He nodded as he scanned the counter behind me. "And whatever smells so good."

"Blueberry muffins." I nodded toward the pan cooling behind me.

"And one of those."

It didn't take me long to whip up his coffee order—which I'd memorized from the first time he was here—and plate his muffin. He nodded toward the small table next to the wall. "Sit with me?" he asked.

I fought the giggle that wanted to emerge, because I

wasn't *that* girl. He pulled out my chair and waited while I set his order down before helping me push it in.

Then he sat on the chair across from me and pulled his coffee and muffin close. He took a few bites before he leaned back in his chair, extending his legs out in front of him and surrounding my chair. "How was your morning?"

I mentally scanned through what I'd done today, making sure to weed out everything that I thought would make me seem extremely boring—or less sexy.

Not quite ready to tell him about Sabrina or Samuel, I moved past that, and the memory of the man at my trunk floated to the front of my mind. That was juicy, and I was kind of interested to see if he was the protective type.

So, I started with the story. By the time I finished, he was done with the muffin. He raised an eyebrow as he pressed the crumbs together and then tossed them into his mouth. "That guy sounds like a creep."

I nodded. "Right?"

Anders sat back, resting his hands on his thighs. "I can come by every morning to make sure you're okay."

I shook my head. As much as I wanted to agree to a full-time bodyguard, I was fine. Sure, this was a small town, but I doubted I would see that man again. "He was probably just a passerby. We get those kinds of people every now and then."

He studied me before he sighed and glanced out the window. "Well, my offer stands."

I smiled. "I appreciate that."

He stared out the window before turning to face me. "I want to ask you something. Will you promise that you'll say yes?"

This was a strange sort of trust game, but I lived a boring life, and I was kind of ready to spice things up.

"Sure?" I asked, making sure to raise my pitch, so he knew that I was nervous about what he was going to say.

He leaned forward and rested his hand on the table right in front of mine. Then he slowly reached forward with his forefinger and brushed my knuckles. "Have a drink with me tonight?"

14

MILES

SWEET TEA &
SOUTHERN GENTLEMAN

I WAS PISSED.

I was furious.

I didn't know what Shelby's angle was, but what she did last night left me fuming.

After Laura went home and Shelby left, I gave Belle a bath, read her a story, and tucked her into bed. Then I spent the rest of the night tossing and turning, trying to sort out why Shelby would interfere with my love life like that.

Did she think I needed help dating?

I stared up at the dark ceiling above me. It was almost dawn, and I could see light starting to spread across the white paint. I had one arm tucked behind my head and the other one resting on my bare chest. I'd pulled off most of my covers because they felt like snakes suffocating me through the night.

I welcomed the cool temperature of my room. It helped lessen the anger I felt toward Shelby and this whole situation.

"What do you want?" I asked to no one in particular as I closed my eyes and Shelby's face drifted into my mind.

When I laid eyes on her six months ago as she pulled up to the funeral home, I had to do a double take. She'd changed, but in a lot of ways, she'd stayed the same. Her figure had filled out, and I couldn't help but swallow when her hips swished past me.

I hated that after all these years, I still loved her. I hated that she hated me. And I hated that there was nothing I could do to change her mind.

Nothing.

I cursed and pulled off the covers resting over my feet. I needed to do something, or I was going to explode. I dressed in my workout shorts and slipped into Belle's room just to make sure she was okay; then I grabbed the monitor and headed to the garage out back.

A good, hard workout would clear my mind. It would help me push out these ridiculous thoughts about Shelby and wake me up.

Once I got to the garage, I pulled open the door and turned on the light. After slipping my earbuds in, I set up the monitor so I could see it and turned on my workout tunes. The beat pulsed through me as I racked my weights for my warmup.

Halfway through my workout, I paused and walked

through the garage to grab a water from the mini fridge. After checking the monitor, I cracked the lid to the water bottle and walked outside. I couldn't see the sun, but its rays were warming the clouds just above the trees.

Tipping the water into my mouth, I scanned the inn. We were pretty empty until Friday. Most of the guests from the weekend had left. Which was nice. When morning came, Shelby would fulfill her commitment to help make breakfast and watch Belle. And, with less work to do, I wouldn't have to be gone that long.

I just had a few rooms that needed fresh sheets and a cleaning. Then I was done and could spend the rest of the day with Belle.

My gaze wandered over to the cottage, and I let myself imagine what Shelby was doing. Was she lying in bed? Was she in those ridiculously thin, short pajamas that she walked into the inn wearing yesterday morning?

Warmth spread through my gut, and I let out an involuntary groan. Then I cursed myself. What was wrong with me? I closed my eyes, and when I opened them, I froze.

Shelby had stepped out of the cottage and was standing on the small porch with a coffee mug in hand. Of course, she had on those tiny pajamas. But they were red this time instead of pink like yesterday. Her hair was pulled back into a messy bun, and I took in the smooth skin of her neck that trailed down to her shoulders.

My fingertips tingled as I wondered what it would feel

like to touch her. To press my lips to the hollow of her neck. Would she gasp? Sigh? Lean into me, beckoning me to kiss her again?

Realizing that I was most definitely staring at a private moment, I dropped my gaze, pushed my hands through my damp hair, and turned back to my workout. These thoughts weren't going to change Shelby's mind, and they most certainly wouldn't help me keep my sanity.

It was like going into battle buck naked and unarmed. If she even caught a whiff of my feelings for her, all bets would be off. She'd purposely break my heart, as opposed to now, where my heart was still broken, but I could fantasize that she could want me someday.

Even though it would always be that—a fantasy—I clung to the possibility of a future with her like it was my life raft and I was drowning.

I zeroed in on my workout bench and laid down on it, arching my back to prep for another set. I spaced my hands evenly on the bar and then pumped my arms a few times, getting them ready to lift the weight.

Right before I lifted the bar off the hooks, I snuck a peek at Shelby, and a slow smile spread across my lips. She was watching me. She was pretending that she wasn't, but she was watching me.

That realization caused blood to pump through my veins. Suddenly, I needed to prove myself to this woman. Call it animalistic. Call it carnal. But I wanted her to see what I could do.

I lifted the bar and started pumping the weights up and down. I didn't stop until my arms felt as if they were going to fall out of their sockets. I racked the weights and shook out my arms and did a second rep. From the corner of my eye, I could see Shelby kept her gaze trained on me, which just spurred me on.

After the third rep, I sat up and grabbed a sweat rag and water. I took a long drink, wiped my forehead, and tossed the rag in the corner. I stood and stretched. I made sure to pass by the monitor, just to make sure Belle hadn't awoken, and then dropped down to the ground to start doing pushups.

I smiled as I could only imagine what Shelby was thinking. She had changed, but so had I.

I was no longer that skinny kid in high school. Exercise helped me deal with the stress in my life. Plus, it helped me feel like a man. I loved my daughter and Charlotte, but between the two of them, everything was pink or covered in doilies and floral print.

This garage. My weights. It was my connection to the man inside of me.

And the fact that the woman I wanted currently had her eyes glued to me, spurred me on in a way that startled even me.

I finished a set of pushups and jumped up, peeking over at Shelby just to make sure she was still watching. I fought a smile as I brought my gaze up fully to meet hers.

Her eyes widened as I allowed a slow smile to spread

across my lips before I gave her a wink and brought my arms up to give her a full flex of my muscles.

When I returned my gaze to her, she'd turned around and hurried into the cottage. I let out a laugh, which helped release all of the tension I had built up inside of me. My muscles were like pudding, but my soul was singing.

From the length of time Shelby had spent watching me, to how embarrassed she was that I'd caught her, one thing was clear.

She was attracted to me.

It may never turn into anything. But for now, I was going to revel in the fact that Shelby had seen my bare chest, and she hadn't turned away.

She'd lingered.

This was like my Christmas and birthday all in one. And, at least for now, I was going to enjoy my gift. Until reality hit me in the face, and I had to come back down to Earth.

When I got back into the inn, I showered and dressed. I was still smiling when I walked into Belle's room to get her ready for the day. She was cooing in her crib as she chewed on her blanket. When she saw me, she giggled and threw her hands up.

I lifted her out to change her diaper and dress her. When she was ready, I clipped her hair back with a pink bow, like Charlotte had taught me, and opened her door.

She led the way into the kitchen, where I lifted her up

and sat her in her high chair. I got her set up with a sippy cup of milk and then headed to the back door. It was time to get started on breakfast, and if Shelby didn't get in here soon, we were going to have some cranky guests.

I jogged down the back stairs and over to the cottage door. I raised my hand to knock, but it swung open, and Shelby was standing there with wide eyes, holding a spatula. She looked equally as startled, and when her gaze met mine, she blinked before stepping back.

"Was that you?"

Confused and on alert that at any moment I could be swatted with a spatula, I raised my hand for protection and said, "Was what me?"

"That noise." She stepped closer, so she could peer out the door, and my senses went haywire.

Everything about her, from the way she smelled, to the way her hair brushed my arm, to the warmth I could feel as she passed by, caused my body to ache with the desire to hold her. I growled and stepped back, needing to put some distance between us.

"I didn't hear anything," I said as I gently took the spatula from her. "But if there was something here, I doubt this would do anything but make it mad."

Her eyes darted around as if she expected bigfoot to jump out from behind a tree, but then she nodded as she let out her breath. "Yeah, you're right. I'm crazy." She rubbed her eyes and then peered over at me. "Why did you come down?"

It might just be the way the sun was hitting her this early in the morning, or maybe she was remembering the show I put on for her, but her gaze drifted down to my chest for a moment, and I swore I saw her cheeks turn pink. I chuckled under my breath but covered it up with a shrug.

"I'm here to get you for breakfast duty."

She glanced over at the inn and then nodded. She disappeared into the cottage and came back out with her sandals. Her hands were tucked into her hoodie, and she was wearing a pair of faded jeans with holes in the knees.

She still looked jumpy but calmer.

I shut her door as she stepped out onto the porch. "I'll install a surveillance camera if that'll make you feel better," I said.

She nodded. We walked in silence to the inn's back door and into the kitchen. Belle was right where I'd put her, but her sippy cup was on the floor. I picked it up and rinsed it off before I handed it back to her.

She giggled and tossed it on the floor. I sighed and tousled her hair. "I guess you're ready for some food."

She babbled while I opened the cereal cupboard and pulled out some of her finger foods to satiate her while I cooked some oatmeal. When I looked up, I caught Shelby staring at me.

I shot her a quizzical look as I started to fill up a pot with water. "What?"

She shrugged as she straightened and began to run her fingers across the countertop. "It's just strange."

I flipped off the water and set the pot onto the stove. I turned, folded my arms, and extended out my feet as I rested against the cupboards behind me. "What is?"

"You. Belle." She waved her hand between the two of us. "The fact that you're a father, and you have a daughter."

"Why is that weird?"

She continued to trace the darker lines in the countertop with her finger. "I guess I just never saw you wanting kids."

I pinched my lips shut at her comment. The truth was, I hadn't wanted kids. After she lost her baby, I realized that children only brought pain. That wasn't something I wanted to voluntarily bring into my life. Belle had been a hard surprise for me. And it made me feel guilty to say that. I wasn't ready to be a father, but I did it anyway. I was happy now.

"Yeah," I said as I scrubbed my face. "Well, it wasn't my first choice. But now I'm grateful I have her." My gaze drifted to my daughter's chubby face as she gleefully shoved the puffs into her mouth.

"And her mom?" Shelby's voice was quiet as if she weren't sure she was allowed to ask.

"Tamara?"

Shelby shrugged. "Is that her name?"

"Yeah." I sighed. "She's gone. Dropped Belle off with

me and split. She got into drugs. Said that having Belle was too much." The water was boiling now, so I turned to dump in the oatmeal. "It's a hard situation, growing up without a mom." I closed my eyes. If anyone knew what that pain was like, it was me. I had always vowed that if I did have kids, I would make sure they had two parents.

I guess I was failing on that front.

"She's lucky she has a dad that cares so much."

Shelby's voice was closer, and when I realized where she was, I pulled back. She'd moved across the kitchen and was now standing next to me, peering into the pot of boiling oatmeal.

Once again, every atom of my body became acutely aware of her presence. I closed my eyes for a moment and inhaled the smell of peaches that wafted up from her hair when she turned her head. When her arm brushed mine, zaps of electricity shot up my arm and exploded in my chest.

"So, what am I making?" she asked, her voice soft and feminine.

I opened my eyes, embarrassed that I'd allowed myself to fall down this rabbit hole. Shelby didn't look the least bit bothered by my presence. It hurt, but it was a good reminder that this was a one-sided love.

"Am I making oatmeal, too?" she asked, tipping her face up to look at me.

I glanced down at her, my gaze slipping down to her

pink lips. They looked soft, and the urge to press my lips against them raced through my body. I clenched my jaw, grounding myself in the present and shrugged. "If you want to."

She studied me, and I worried that she'd seen me staring at her mouth. Heat pricked at the back of my neck, and I knew I needed to step back. I needed to put some space between us. If I didn't, I feared that I might throw caution to the wind and kiss her.

Which would destroy everything I'd worked so hard for.

Shelby didn't want to be here, but I'd promised her that when she arrived, I'd stay away from her so she would feel comfortable. I'd thought that meant she would hole up in the cottage, but she surprised me that first morning and came out. She surprised me again when she agreed to her grandmother's stipulations and was even willing to help around the inn.

Shelby was making steps in a positive direction, and the last thing I wanted to do was scare her off.

"If I want to," she whispered as she glanced around the kitchen. She had grabbed a wooden spoon and was gently slapping it against her palm. I could see that she was in deep thought, which helped calm me down.

If she was aware of my attraction to her, I was certain she would let me know. For now, she was clueless, and I was going to keep it that way.

Belle's oatmeal was finished, so I poured it into a bowl, added brown sugar and blueberries, and then pulled up a chair next to her, blowing at the steam rising from the bowl. Shelby was moving around the kitchen, and I couldn't help but watch her. My heart pounded when she passed by me, bumping me with her hip.

I turned to say something quippy, but nothing came out. My mouth turned dry as I forced my gaze back to my daughter. If I let my thoughts continue down this path, I was just going to make myself more miserable.

And that cup already runneth over.

"What are you making?" I asked, focusing on my daughter as I fed her. I forced my gaze to stay trained on Belle's chubby face.

"Pancakes," she said.

The soft, excited tone of her voice drew my attention over to her despite my best efforts. "Pancakes?"

She nodded, whipping the spatula around above her. "It's going to be magnificent." Her words ended in a small smile.

I laughed, taking in the flour that she'd already managed to smear across her cheek. I stood and grabbed a dish towel I'd set on the oven's handle earlier and closed the space between us. I pressed my forefinger to the bottom of her chin and tipped her face toward me before I took the dish towel and rubbed her cheek.

Her whole body stilled as her gaze moved slowly to

meet mine. She looked startled—not scared—but it was in her hesitation that I realized what I'd just done.

My eyes widened, but I forced myself to be calm. "You had some flour there," I said as I dropped my hands and stepped back.

Her eyes were wide, and she brought her hand up to her cheek. "I did?" she whispered.

I nodded and returned the towel. I shrugged even though my entire body felt alive with electricity. Touching Shelby had been a mistake, but I wouldn't take it back even if I could. Her skin was soft and warm. Every part of her called out to me in a way that my body could never ignore. "I guess it's a hazard of the trade," I said as I moved to sit down next to Belle.

"What is?"

I glanced over at Shelby before nodding in Belle's direction. "Taking care of people. Once a dad, always a dad." I returned to feeding Belle, keeping my gaze stuck in one place.

I hoped Shelby bought my explanation. Me wiping her cheek was just a result of me wiping Belle's face forever. It had nothing to do with my constant desire to be close to her.

Moments later, she was moving around the kitchen once more, whipping up the pancake batter and humming to herself. I let myself breathe as she worked, confident that we'd moved on. I needed to check myself in the future

—that was too close. The last thing Shelby needed to know was that I was in love with her.

And after touching her—being close to her—one thing was for sure.

I could never walk away from her.

15

SHELBY

SWEET TEA &
SOUTHERN GENTLEMAN

THE MORNING'S events had been strange, and I was still trying to process what had happened as I plunged my hands into the soapy dishwater after breakfast. Miles had served the guests my pancakes and the sausage he'd made after he fed Belle. All the while, I made sure to stay far away from him.

After being caught watching him as he worked out, I still thought I could handle myself in the kitchen. But my heart pounded in my chest when he innocently wiped flour from my cheek.

He was a dad, and it was cute that being a dad wasn't something he could compartmentalize. He was protective. And there was something about the way he insisted on being protective of me that made my whole body feel light.

It was probably because I never had a dad in my life.

"It has to be," I whispered as I grabbed the mixing

bowl, tipped it on its side, and watched as the water flooded over the rim.

"What has to be?"

I yelped and turned. Miles's voice had scared the living daylights out of me. He was standing behind me with Belle perched on his arm. He'd taken her to the bathroom to clean the oatmeal from her hair. She smiled at me with her hair sticking up from the water.

I smiled back at her, wiping my hand on my hoodie before I reached forward to smooth down her hair. "Does daddy not know how to do your hair?" I asked as I combed my fingers through the snarls.

Suddenly, I realized just how close I was to Miles. He was staring at me. The look in his eyes was cloudy, and I wasn't sure how to read it. Not letting it confuse me, I finished fixing Belle's hair and turned my attention back to the dishes.

The heat of the water in the sink, plus the heat that had started creeping up on me when Miles neared, made me slip off my hoodie. I was wearing a black tank underneath, and as soon as the cool air hit my bare arms, my body began to relax.

That had been my problem; I was just warm.

"I'll have you know that I *do* know how to do Belle's hair," Miles said as he moved to stand next to me. He'd let Belle down and pulled out a basket of kitchen toys that she was content playing with.

I knew I shouldn't, but despite the warning bells

sounding in my mind, I glanced up at him. "You do?" I asked and then turned my attention back to the bowl and began washing it.

"Yes. Charlotte made sure I knew how to fix it right." His arm brushed mine as he moved to take the bowl from my hands and turned on the water.

Warmth traveled across my skin from his touch, but I was too distracted with the mention of my grandmother to focus on my reaction. "She did?" I whispered, my whole body stilling as if to use its entire energy focusing on what Miles had said.

Miles set down the bowl and towel and then rested his hands on the counter. I didn't have to say anything to know that we were both thinking the same thing. There was enough history between the two of us to last a lifetime. And here we were, young and battling the decisions our parents made so long ago.

The decisions that left us to be raised by an elderly woman.

"She missed you, you know," he said. His voice was deep and steeped in emotion.

Tears pricked my eyes. "No, she didn't." How could she? I'd said horrible things. I'd done horrible things. I'd run away. She had died without me here. I'd resent any person who did that to me. Like I resented my mother.

"She regretted what she said that night." Miles's voice was barely a whisper now. I could feel his gaze on my face, but I couldn't bring myself to look up.

I didn't know what to say. I never willingly allowed myself to think about that night or the pain that I felt. I'd been alone and broken with no one around to fix me. A tear slipped down my cheek, and I hurried to wipe it away. "Please stop," I choked out.

Miles didn't answer. I closed my eyes and tipped my body away from the sink so I could lean against the cupboard next to me. I covered my face with my hands and welcomed the darkness. My knees felt like they were going to give way, so I slid down until I rested firmly on the floor.

I wasn't ready for this. I wasn't ready to face the past that haunted me in the middle of the night. My history here was like a big gaping wound in my heart, and even though I wanted to say that I was fixed...I wasn't.

And I wasn't ever going to be.

Suddenly, someone grabbed my hand and started to pull my fingers from my face. Thinking it was Miles, I dropped my hands, but it wasn't him. Instead, I was staring into the wide and concerned eyes of Belle. Her chubby hand held onto my fingers. Her eyebrows were furrowed.

An uncontrollable sob escaped my lips, which only made her stick out her tiny bottom lip. Not wanting to make a toddler cry, I wrapped my arms around her and held her against my chest. She wrapped her tiny arms around my neck and squeezed.

Even though I was broken beyond repair, something

happened between us. She couldn't say much, but I could feel her worry for me, and it helped. It helped a lot.

"I'm sorry for making you sad," I whispered as I brought my hand up to her head and held her against my shoulder.

We sat there for as long as Belle let me hold her. When she started to wiggle and push away, I let her go. I felt calmer as she waddled back over to her toys and started playing with them again.

Taking in a deep breath, I moved to stand, only to have Miles's hand appear in front of me. I thought about swatting it away, but he was just trying to help. I didn't need to be a brat about it.

"Thanks," I said, slipping my hand into his and letting him help me up.

He nodded and handed me a tissue. I wiped my eyes and nose and then crumpled the tissue and looked around.

"Behind you," Miles said.

After tossing the tissue in the garbage, I took in a deep breath. I could feel Miles watching me, but I didn't want to talk about it. Instead, I turned, grabbed the dishrag, and continued washing.

We worked in silence; the only sounds were the low murmur of voices coming from the dining room and Belle's soft singing.

The energy between the two of us was palpable, but I pushed it aside. Once I was done, I rinsed off the sink and went to grab a towel, only to have Miles hand me one. I hesitated but took it, wiping my hands dry and setting it down on the counter behind me.

"If you don't mind, I'm going to go into town to get some coffee. When I get back, I can watch Belle." I gathered my courage and glanced up to meet his gaze.

He had his eyebrows drawn together, and I could tell that he wanted to say something. I just gave him a small smile, hoping he'd move on.

"That's fine," he said as he folded his arms across his chest and leaned back against the counter.

"Great." I grabbed my hoodie and started toward the back door, making sure to ruffle Belle's hair as I went. She glanced up at me with a plastic toy spoon in her mouth and grinned. "I'll see you later, squirt."

Just as I pulled open the back door, Miles's voice stopped me.

"Shelb?"

I winced at the nickname he and Gran used to call me. "Yeah?" I called over my shoulder. I was almost out the door, and I was ready to breathe.

"I'm sorry. I didn't mean to make you cry. I just wanted..."

I paused, stilling my body.

"I just want to make you happy."

I closed my eyes for a moment. I understood where he was coming from, but he couldn't fix the past. No one could.

"It's okay. But I'm not sure I'm capable of being happy

THE INN ON HARMONY ISLAND   187

like I used to be." I stepped out onto the deck and shut the door behind me.

I cleared my mind of all thoughts as I crossed the yard, and once I was in the cottage, I slipped into the shower. Fifteen minutes of hot water beating on my back made me feel better.

I toweled dry, dressed, threw my wet hair up into a bun, and gathered my purse. I was going to head into town to get some coffee from Abigail. She was the only one in town who felt like a friend, and I needed a break.

I needed some girl time.

The drive into town was peaceful, and the bookstore was quiet when I walked up to it. I could see Abigail moving around inside as I passed by the window, and I crossed my fingers that she was open. The sign said "Open" when I walked up, but I knocked gently on the window anyway. I was in need of girl talk, and if she was busy, I didn't want to bother her.

That got Abigail's attention. She glanced up and smiled as soon as she saw me. I gave her a small wave, and she motioned toward the oven. I nodded and pulled open the door. The shop looked quiet, so I walked toward the back. Abigail pulled out a cookie sheet, set it down on the counter, and wiped her hands on her apron as I stepped up.

"Sorry to bother you," I said, suddenly realizing that I was being rude, hoping that I hadn't misread our relationship and she was fine with me just randomly popping in.

"Oh, I'm not bothered. I'm actually happy to have someone to talk to while I work." She yawned. "And keep me awake."

"Late night or early morning?" I asked as I followed after her.

She smiled at me as she rounded the corner of the counter and picked up her mug. "Both?"

"Both?" I slipped onto a barstool so I could lean my elbow on the counter and rest my chin in my hand. "You're a party animal."

"Yeah, partying with an infant."

I furrowed my brow. "You have a baby?"

She shook her head as she lifted the mug to her lips and took a sip. "My nephew."

"Ah." I fiddled with the container full of tiny sugar packets in front of me. "They live with you?"

"Mmhmm," Abigail said. Then she set her coffee down. "Can I get you some?" She motioned toward her mug.

"Yes, please." I'd planned on eating breakfast after doing the dishes at the inn. But after my breakdown, I'd lost my appetite.

She poured me a mug and handed it over. After I sugared it up, I took a sip. The warm liquid filled my stomach.

"Can I interest you in a scone?" She motioned toward the cookie sheet she'd just taken out of the oven.

My mouth watered. "They smell amazing."

She smiled as she served me one on a plate. "My grandma's recipe," she said as she handed it over.

I took a bite, and the taste of cinnamon and apple filled my mouth. I moaned and closed my eyes. "This is sinful."

She laughed. "I'm glad you think so."

I didn't stop until the entire scone was gone. Then I grabbed a napkin and wiped my fingers. Abigail was mixing something together in a bowl, and I suddenly felt guilty.

"I'm so sorry," I said, suddenly feeling like a complete idiot.

She furrowed her brow. "For what?"

"We have a completely unbalanced relationship. I come here, you feed me, I leave."

She laughed. "Well, you also pay me." Then she stopped and stared at me. "You're going to pay me, right?"

"Of course." I fumbled for my purse.

She waved her hand. "I was joking. I know you'll pay."

Relief flooded my body, but I pulled a twenty out of my wallet for good measure. I tucked the bill under my plate.

"Did they run out of food at the inn?" she asked as she started cracking eggs into whatever she was making.

I sighed. "No. I just...needed to get away."

She studied me for a moment. I knew that she knew about my past, but I appreciated that she wasn't asking me outright. For this town, that was a miracle. Most people were not shy about wanting to know what was going on with you. Privacy was not a big commodity here.

"Miles was..." I paused, not sure what I was going to say. What was Miles? How could I put into words our history?

"A guy?" she offered.

I glanced over at her. She was smiling. Thankful for the nondescript answer, I nodded. "Yeah, a guy."

She sighed as she left the bowl she was holding and headed to a drawer to grab a cookie scoop. "They always are the root of all our problems."

I nodded and brought my feet up onto the footrest of the stool next to me. "They really are."

She laughed as she scooped what I could only assume was cookie dough onto the sheet in front of her. "So, what did Miles do?"

I pushed some crumbs around on the counter as I chewed on the words I wanted to say. Giving up, I decided that the most direct way was probably the best. "He worked out in the garage today."

She stopped scooping the dough and turned to look at me. "And that's bad?"

I groaned and covered my face with my hands. "Well, yeah. When he does it shirtless and he's like..." I scrunched up my face. What was I saying? And why was I saying it out loud? Abigail was going to think I was a crazy person and kick me out of her shop.

"Ah," she said, and I could hear the laughter in her voice.

I dropped my hands and looked at her. "What?"

Her lips were pinched together in a tight smile, as if she were trying to hide that she was laughing at me.

"What?" I asked again.

She shrugged. "I take it Miles has changed since you saw him last."

I tipped my head back and closed my eyes. The answer was, yes, he had. He'd changed a lot. But it wasn't only in his physical appearance. It was everything. He was sweet. Kind. He loved Belle like she was the only important thing in his life.

And he cared about me.

"I don't know. Maybe it's just been so long since I've been around a decent guy that I guess..." I groaned and buried my face in the crook of my elbow.

"It's okay." Abigail's voice was close. I peeked over my arm to see that she was standing in front of me now. "You don't have to unpack anything for me."

I straightened and shot her a smile. "Thanks." I needed that. I needed the freedom to just let things lie. I didn't want to have to try to figure out why I was feeling the way I was. The truth was, I didn't know.

I wasn't sure I was ever going to know.

I stuck around, making small chat with Abigail, for about an hour longer before a group of construction workers came in and Abigail got too busy to talk to me. I gave her a quick wave as I pushed through the front door, but she had her hands full and was only able to offer me a quick nod.

I climbed into my car, and when I turned off of Main Street and started down the road back to the inn, smoke began to billow from Rhonda. I managed to make it to the shoulder before she sputtered and died.

I cursed and unbuckled my seat belt as I climbed out and rounded the hood. I had to keep my distance as smoke continued to fill the air.

"Great," I muttered, bending down to see what was under the car, like that was going to tell me what was wrong. Feeling ridiculous, I glanced down the way I'd come. Then I peered down the way I was going.

The only person who came to mind was Miles. I wasn't sure if I wanted to call him. Then I shook my head. I was being ridiculous. I was going to call Miles, he was going to come pick me up, and when I got to the inn, he was going to give me some advice on who to call to come pick up my car.

It wasn't rocket science.

I pulled my phone out of my back pocket and found Miles's number. I pressed on it and waited.

"Hello?"

"Miles?"

He paused. "Shelby?"

"I need your help."

"What happened?" Butterflies erupted in my stomach

at the protective way he said those words. *Crap. Focus, Shelby.*

"Rhonda is billowing smoke."

"Rhonda?"

"My car.

"Oh. Where are you?"

"About ten minutes down Whipporwillow."

"Gotcha. I'll pack up Belle, and we'll head your way."

He didn't give me any time to say anything else before he hung up, so I slipped my phone back into my pocket and went back to my car. I was leaning against Rhonda with my purse hooked over my shoulder when Miles showed up. He gave me a quick three finger wave as he pulled in, and I pushed off the car.

"Yeesh," he said as he jumped out of his truck

"Yeah," I said, meeting him at the hood of my car. Thankfully, it wasn't smoking as bad as before.

"When was the last time you had an oil change?"

I chewed my lip. "I don't know."

He peered over at me. He was only a foot or so away from me, and despite my best effort, my body made me very aware of this fact. "That's not good, Shelb."

I pinched the bridge of my nose between my thumb and forefinger. "I know."

"Your car is most likely dead." He bumped me with his shoulder. "Like, for good."

"I know what dead means," I said as I dropped my hand to where he'd touched me.

"Well, let's get you back to the inn and into some air conditioning, and we'll call Ralph." He turned and nodded to his truck.

"Perfect." I followed behind him as he made his way to the passenger door and pulled it open. He held out his hand, and I took it as he helped me climb into the seat. Pops of electricity raced through my whole body from his touch, and when his fingers lingered on mine for a second longer than normal, I glanced down at him.

If he had the same reaction, he didn't show it. He waited for me to situate myself before he shut my door, jogged around the hood, and climbed in. I glanced to the back to see Belle holding her foot as she stared out her window.

"Let's go, m'ladies," Miles said as he put his truck in drive and started down the road to the inn.

I watched as his hands rested on the steering wheel. I knew I should pull my gaze away, but I couldn't. Especially when I noticed that he had paint on the back of his hand.

"What's that?" I asked before I could stop myself.

Miles looked over at me. "What's what?" He followed my gaze and opened and closed his hand a few times. "Oh, the paint?"

"Yeah."

He nodded toward his daughter. "Belle and I were painting princesses before I had to come be your knight in shining armor."

"Oh."

He shrugged as he reached back and tickled her foot. "Weren't we, Belle?" She giggled, and my heart began to race in my chest.

I hated that Miles was so sweet with Belle. I hated that he was so quick to rescue me and didn't make me feel stupid for my car breaking down.

I hated that, perhaps, I didn't hate him as much as I thought I did.

It made me vulnerable. Without anger and pain filling my chest, a void had been created. I feared what would try to fill that void.

I wasn't ready to have feelings for any man.

Much less Miles.

16

ABIGAIL

SWEET TEA &
SOUTHERN GENTLEMAN

I WAS NERVOUS.

I felt stupid for being nervous, but I was.

I stood in the living room, staring out at the road, waiting for Anders to show up. He texted that he would pick me up at seven, but it was now ten past the hour, and he still wasn't here. Sabrina was snoozing on the couch, and Samuel was asleep in his crib. I estimated that I had about three hours before Samuel woke up, so the clock was ticking.

Suddenly, headlights shone from down the road, and I held my breath. A black truck came into view and then slowed as it rolled up to the front of the apartment building.

My heart pounded as I shouldered my purse and headed to the front door. I didn't want to wake up Sabrina, and I certainly didn't want to wake up Samuel, so I took care in shutting the door behind me before I took off down the hall to the front door.

Anders gave me a small wave from the passenger window as I hurried to the passenger door and pulled on the handle.

"Hey," he said as he took a moment to admire my outfit.

I'd taken my time getting ready, picking the perfect black dress that had been tucked away in my closet, slipping into some red heels, and curling my hair just right.

If he wanted to take a second and appreciate my hard work, I was going to let him.

"Hey," I said as I twisted to grab the seatbelt and click it in place.

"You look..." His whistle finished his sentence.

My cheeks warmed, which was a contrast to the shivers running across my body. It had been so long since I'd been admired like this, that my muscles seemed to be shaking off their slumber and basking in the warmth of his gaze.

I shook my head slightly at that thought as he pulled away from the curb and headed down the street. My entire body began to relax as he drove.

"So, are we going to Harmony Pub?" I asked.

He shook his head. "Actually, I was thinking that we could go back to my place and have a drink."

I quirked an eyebrow. I wasn't sure how I felt about that. I wasn't the kind of girl that just went back to a guy's apartment on the first date. But it did sound nice to sit somewhere quiet and talk. The pub would be crowded, and I always felt like I had to scream to be heard.

"Where do you live?" I glanced over to see he was resting his wrist on the steering wheel and had his other hand resting on his thigh.

"Just past your shop, actually. I'm renting an apartment from Kevin."

I nodded. Kevin, the son of Marcus Proctor. They owned much of the town and acted like royalty here. I didn't run in their circle, but I heard a lot of gossip about them from Missy.

"Kevin and I go way back. We were roommates in college."

"Oh?" That was interesting.

"Yeah. He was smarter than me, though. I dropped out second semester and started doing construction to pay the bills." He pulled in behind the apartment complex on the far side of town and turned off the engine. "I'm here now, though." He leaned closer to me, and the warmth of his body washed over me. "So, I'm not complaining."

His meaning wasn't lost on me as I unbuckled and moved to climb out of the truck. He did the same, and soon, we were walking side by side to the back door of the building.

The feeling of fingers touching the inner part of my forearm startled me, and I glanced down, watching as Anders slid his hand into mine and entwined his fingers with my fingers.

Warmth emanated throughout my entire body as I tried to keep my smile from getting out of hand. There was no need for him to discover that I had basically lived as a nun for the last few years.

He led the way through the building, making sure to hold doors open, and kept the elevator door from shutting on me. I loved how his arm brushed mine as we moved or the way he stood close to me as we waited in the elevator.

He smelled amazing, and I felt tiny in his presence.

"Now, don't judge me when we get in my apartment. I'm a guy, and so is my roommate. We're not dirty, just..." He blew out his breath. "Just guys."

I brought my free hand up to his elbow and held it as I leaned in. "I'm sure it's fine." After all, I lived with Sabrina. That girl could go days without washing a single dish.

His gaze moved down to my hand on his arm before making its way back to meet mine. He smiled and shoved his key into the lock. He flipped on a light and pulled me through the door into his small apartment.

It was small, but clean. The furniture was sparse. Only a futon and coffee table filled the living room. On the far wall was a gigantic TV.

Typical.

The kitchen had some dishes in the sink, and there was a faint smell of Chinese food, like it had just been warmed in the microwave a few minutes ago.

"Huh, Sebastian must be home."

I turned to look at him. "Sebastian?"

"My roommate," he said as he stepped closer. I thought he wanted to be near me, but then I heard the front door shut behind me. "It's fine. He shouldn't bother us."

I chewed my lip as I glanced around. It was actually better that way. After all, I'd just met Anders. Having a second person here helped me feel more comfortable.

"What can I get you to drink?" he asked as he let go of my hand and moved to set his keys down in a small bowl on the kitchen counter.

I felt lonely without my hand in his, so I moved to follow him. "Umm, what do you have?" I asked as he pulled open the fridge.

His back was so broad that I couldn't see inside as he leaned into it. When he straightened, he had a bottle of wine in his hand. "How about some of this?" he asked.

I quirked an eyebrow. "This is expensive," I said as I took it from him.

He shrugged. "It's Bash's. I'm pretty sure he won't mind if we drink some."

I stepped back as I held the bottle and Anders moved to grab some glasses from the cupboard. "Bash is rich?"

Anders looked at me from over his shoulder. "Does wealth matter to you?"

I gave him a soft smile. "Absolutely not." I looked around. "It's just that if he's rich, why don't you live somewhere else?"

Anders stepped up to me with two glasses in his hands. He set them down on the counter next to him and then took the bottle of wine, setting it next to the glasses before he stepped closer. His body was barely an inch from mine.

I was still too scared to look up at him. I worried that if I did, he would see the fear in my gaze. I hadn't done this in so long...would I mess it up?

"Abigail?" He said it like he was enjoying the way my name tasted on his lips.

"Yeah?" I breathed out as I closed my eyes. My entire body felt tight as I waited for what he was going to do.

"Will you look at me?"

I slowly let out my breath as I tipped my face up. His forefinger found the bottom of my chin, and he pressed. Suddenly I was staring into his warm, brown eyes. The amount of desire I saw in his gaze took my breath away.

"You look amazing tonight," he murmured as he gently pressed his lips to my collarbone.

A small moan escaped my lips before I could stop it. I pinched my lips together as I widened my eyes. Anders must have heard because he pulled back and tipped his lips up into a smile.

"I'm sorry," I whispered.

He shook his head. "Don't ever feel embarrassed to express your pleasure." He brushed his lips against my cheek as he brought them closer to my ear. "Especially if I'm the one giving it to you."

Warmth filled my stomach as I tipped my face and crushed my lips against his. He chuckled and wrapped his arms around my waist, pulling me against him. My hands slid from his shoulders to the nape of his neck as I clung to him. His lips were warm as they moved across mine.

He teased my lips with his tongue, and I responded by parting them. He tasted like cinnamon as he explored my mouth. His hands found my hips, and he bent down, cupping my rear. Before I knew it, he'd lifted me up. I responded by wrapping my legs around him as he set me down on the counter.

I was now higher than him, so I rested my hands on his shoulders before I slid them forward, caging him in with my arms. His hands found the small of my back and dragged upwards before he pulled me closer to him.

I wanted every part of my body to touch him.

I wasn't sure how long we were in the kitchen, kissing, but by the time he pulled back, my lips felt swollen, and my gaze was foggy as I attempted to focus on him. His cocky smile was back as he rested his hands on my now exposed thighs, drawing circles with his fingers.

"That was amazing," he said as he leaned forward and pressed his lips against mine once more.

"It was," I said, responding with another kiss.

He chuckled against my lips before pulling back.

I moaned, disappointed that he was leaving.

"I gotta use the bathroom." He pulled back. "Stay right here."

I pointed to the floor in front of me and gave him a small salute. He laughed as he gave me a wink and then turned and headed down the hallway to the left of the kitchen. I sat on the counter, glancing around.

I didn't move to pull my dress down. I would only have to hike it back up when he came back. I was fairly certain I wasn't done kissing Anders, and I had a suspicion that he wasn't done kissing me either.

With my hands on either side of me, I sighed as I kicked my feet. I pressed my lips together and smiled, reveling in the memory of kissing Anders.

I brought my fingers to my lips and touched them. The memory of Anders' lips on mine warmed my heart.

I heard a door open in the hallway that Anders had disappeared down, and the sound got my heart pumping again. I fluffed my hair and wiped under my eyes as I prepped for his return.

I kept my face tipped so that I could see if he was coming, but also, so it didn't look like I was too eager. A figure appeared in the hallway, and just as I turned to smile, my entire body froze.

I was staring into the bright blue eyes of the man that had been digging around in my trunk yesterday.

"You?" I asked as I raised my finger and pointed at him.

He blinked a few times before his gaze dropped to my exposed legs. Realizing the compromising situation I was currently in, I slipped off the counter, pulling my skirt down as far as I could.

"What are you doing in my apartment?" he asked, glancing behind me. I followed his gaze to see that he was staring at the wine and glasses. "Oh, never mind. Anders?" he yelled over his shoulder.

Another door opened, and Anders suddenly appeared next to him. "Hey, man. I didn't know you were going to be home tonight." Anders clapped his hand on his shoulder. "Did you meet Abigail?"

The man's eyes shot over to me. "Abigail?"

"Yep. She runs the bookstore-slash-coffee-heaven in town." He chuckled. "The place I'm always running off to early in the morning."

The man's eyes narrowed. "What is she doing here?"

Anders frowned as he studied the man and then glanced over to me. "I invited her."

He looked over at Anders, and I could feel his glare. "You should've let me know."

"Geez, Bash. I didn't think you'd care."

Bash. This was the roommate, Sebastian. That was his name. Ha. At least I knew it now.

Bash looked over at me and then back to Anders and growled—actually growled—before he turned and stormed back into his room. I watched him go until I could no longer see him and then turned my attention to Anders. He looked just as confused as I felt when he turned back to study me.

"What's gotten into him?"

I shrugged as I leaned against the counter. "I don't know." I decided to keep my and Bash's little run-in at my store secret for now. It was already apparent that he didn't like me. I didn't need him feeding Anders any weird information about the conversation we had as I chased him down the street.

From the looks of it, Bash wanted nothing to do with me, and I wanted nothing to do with him. As long as he stayed away from me, I was going to stay away from him.

It was a win-win.

Thankfully, the effect of Bash's sour mood quickly dissipated as Anders sauntered over to me and slid his hands from my waist to my back before resting them on the counter behind me. He leaned in and nuzzled my neck.

"Where were we?" he asked.

I giggled, wrapping my arms around his neck and tipping my head back, as he gently pressed his lips from the hollows of my neck to the back of my ear.

"Oh, that's right. We were right here," he said, his voice so low and sexy that my entire body responded.

His lips found mine, and I fell back into kissing him. It was as easy as breathing.

Here, I was happy. For the first time in a long time, I was doing something for me. And there wasn't anything that was going to stop me. Not Sabrina. Not Samuel.

And certainly not Anders's grumpy, sullen roommate.

I was going to enjoy myself tonight if it was the last thing I did.

SWEET TEA &
SOUTHERN GENTLEMAN

BELLE.

My entire body tightened as I sat straight up in bed before turning to grab the monitor. I could hear my daughter's cries before I opened my eyes. Grabbing my comforter, I ripped it off and jumped out of bed.

Something was wrong. This wasn't her normal cry.

I stumbled into her room, flipping on the nightstand light as I passed by.

"Hey, hey," I whispered as I peered down into her crib.

She was lying on her back, with tears streaming down her bright pink cheeks. I lifted her out of the crib and brought her to my shoulder where she cried into my neck. She was warm.

I walked out of her room and into the bathroom. I didn't need a thermometer to know what I already knew.

She had a fever. After digging around in the bathroom closet at a strange angle because I wanted to keep her as comfortable as I could, I found the thermometer but not the baby fever reducer.

I cursed quietly. I'd used it all up when she went through a bad teething episode last month. Holding her head to my shoulder to keep her from slipping off, I made my way back into my room and sat on the bed. She was compliant and let me press the thermometer to her forehead.

Her cry had turned to a whimper as she snuggled into my neck. Once the thermometer beeped, I pulled it down and glanced at the screen.

102.3

It was high, but it wasn't too high. Even though all I wanted to do was pack her into the truck and take her to the hospital, I could hear Charlotte in my ear: "She'll catch more disease by bringing her in with her immune system already struggling than if you just kept her here and nursed her yourself."

I knew a fever was cause for worry but not alarm. I just needed some fever reducer to help her feel better.

Shelby.

I glanced around my room for my phone and found it sitting on my nightstand, plugged in. I leaned over the bed and grabbed it. Once I wiggled the charging cable from the phone, I took it, plus the blanket on my bed, and made my way out to the living room.

I sat on the couch with Belle on my chest and my feet up on the coffee table. With her situated and comfortable for now, I powered on my phone and scrolled through my contacts.

I pressed talk as soon as I found Shelby's name and then brought the phone to my cheek. It took a few rings before she answered.

"Hello?" Her voice was low and breathy.

"I need your help."

"Miles?"

I closed my eyes. The sound of my name in her sleepy voice stirred things inside of me. This wasn't the time or the place to dwell on any of those thoughts. "Yeah. It's Belle."

"Belle?" Her voice was more alert now. "What's wrong? Is she okay? Do you need me to come over?"

"She has a fever. She'll probably be fine, but I'm out of fever reducer."

"Do you need me to go get some?"

"Yes. Please."

I could hear rustling in the background. A second later, she cursed and then said, "I just stubbed my toe."

I straightened a little. "Slow down then. We'll be here. We're fine." A surge of protection coursed through my chest. "I don't need you getting into an accident or anything because you were in too much of a hurry. Keys are in the glove compartment in the truck. It should start right up for you."

She let out a soft, mmhmm before saying, "I'll be as quick as I can."

I hesitated, fighting the desire to tell her once again that I didn't want her to chance hurting herself, but she hung up before I could say anything. I dropped my phone down on the couch next to me and contemplated calling her back, but I didn't want to distract her if she was on the road already.

I lay there on the couch with Belle finally snoozing on my chest, waiting. Waiting for the sound of the door to open. Waiting to hear her footsteps on the hardwood floors. Waiting for her to tell me she got back safe.

I must have dozed off, but the sound of the medicine bottle being set down on the coffee table woke me up. I glanced over to see Shelby slowly turning away from me as if she were trying as hard as she could to be quiet. I watched her take a step toward the door, relief filling my chest that she'd made it back.

As if she knew I was watching her, she glanced over her shoulder and met my gaze. Then she winced like she felt bad about waking me, but I didn't care. I loved that she went out for Belle. I loved that she was worried the moment I told her something was wrong. And I loved that she didn't want to wake me up.

I just loved...her.

"Stay," I whispered before I could stop myself.

Her eyes widened, and I suddenly worried that I'd done the wrong thing. She didn't know how I felt about her, and this might be the moment that she discovered my true feelings.

It felt like an eternity, but eventually, she nodded and slipped off her purse. She disappeared for a moment and came back, padding over to me in her socks. She stood next to me like she didn't know what to do, so I lifted my arm and motioned for her to sit.

She hesitated as she glanced between the spot on the couch and me. I knew I should feel guilty, taking advantage of the fact that my daughter was sick. But I didn't care. I needed this.

Bad.

Finally, Shelby sat down next to me. Luckily, I weighed more than her, and with the way the couch cushions were situated, her body tipped into mine. I dropped my arm on her shoulder and inhaled the smell of her shampoo.

"Is this okay?" she asked as she pulled back a bit like she was about to shift away.

"Don't," I whispered as I closed my eyes, gripping my hand on her shoulder.

"Miles," she whispered.

I had to bite back my groan. She needed to stop speaking. She needed to stop moving. She needed to stop being so dang sexy. This wasn't the time or the place for my mind to wander.

"Just sit here with me," I said, my voice low. My ability to hide my feelings for her slipping away.

She tensed for a moment before I felt her entire body relax. Every molecule of my body was acutely aware of where her body pressed to mine, but she didn't seem as bothered. Eventually, I heard her breathing deepen, and her head became heavy on my shoulder.

With Belle on my chest and Shelby next to me, my chest swelled. This was perfection. I couldn't ask for anything more than these two women in my life.

I wanted this.

I wanted Shelby. I wanted Belle. And I wanted us to be a family.

I turned my head, so I could gently kiss the top of Shelby's head. With her next to me, but not awake, I could finally show her my affection without her walking away.

Without her rejecting me.

I kept my lips on her head as I whispered, "I love you. And someday, I'll tell you that."

I closed my eyes and said a small prayer in my mind that, someday, she'd be willing to hear those words leave my lips.

I wasn't sure how long I sat there, but I must have eventually fallen asleep. I awoke the next morning with my neck aching from the angle I'd slept in. I shifted my body slightly; my muscles were numb from sitting on the couch the whole night.

Realizing that I couldn't fully move because of weight next to me, I turned to see that Shelby was still asleep. Belle must have moved in the night, because she was sleeping on the other half of the couch right next to me.

But Shelby was still sleeping right on my chest with my arm wrapped around her shoulders. She hadn't gotten up.

She hadn't left.

I must have still been hazy from sleep, because I placed a kiss on her head once more and murmured, "You stayed," into her hair. I smiled as I closed my eyes, reveling in this feeling and knowing, in a short amount of time, she was going to leave. She was going to wake up and realize that she was still sitting here next to me. And being here was the last place she wanted to be.

I felt her begin to stir and worried that she'd heard me or felt me kiss her head. I dropped my head back against the couch and closed my eyes. I lay there, waiting to see what she was going to do. Suddenly, her weight lessened, and I could tell from the way the couch cushions were shifting, she was trying to get up as quietly as possible.

Not wanting her to leave, and stupidly thinking that if she knew I was waking up, she would stay, I pulled my head up and blinked a few times. Her face was veiled by her hair as she sat on the edge of the couch.

"Thanks," I whispered.

She startled, pulling the curtain of her hair back and staring at me with wide eyes. "For what?" she asked. Her voice was incredibly sexy in the morning.

"For getting Belle some medicine," I said as I dropped

my hand to my daughter's forehead and felt for the fever that had ravaged her body last night. I was relieved when her temperature felt normal. I'd waited for her to wake up again to give her some medicine, but she never had, and I didn't want to disturb my sleeping girl.

"Of course," she said as she reached over, grabbed her shoe, and started wiggling her foot into it.

"And for staying last night." My voice was low and full of emotion. Sure, I should have tried to hide my appreciation, but I was tired of doing that. I wanted—needed—her to know how I felt, even if I couldn't say the words out loud.

Her entire body froze. Her fingers were stuffed into the back of her shoe as she'd been trying to pull it on without having to loosen her laces. "Of course," she repeated. "I'd do anything for that little girl. Even staying here...on the couch."

I tried not to read too much into her words, but I couldn't help it. Staying here had nothing to do with me and everything to do with Belle. I couldn't blame her for that. After all, my daughter had a tendency to win a lot of hearts. But I was selfish, and I wanted some hint, some tiny crack in the armor around Shelby, to show that my feelings might eventually be reciprocated.

I was an idiot and a fool. I should move on. I should get over her. But no matter how many times I told myself that, I couldn't seem to walk away.

"I'll let her know of your brave actions when she

wakes up," I said as I watched Shelby stand and wiggle her foot until it sunk safely into her shoe.

"You do that," she said, pushing her hair from her face and giving me a quick smile. "I'm going to head back since you seem to have it under control here." She grabbed her purse and pulled it up onto her shoulder.

"Okay." The couch felt cold and empty without her.

"I'll shower and come back over to help with breakfast."

I shook my head. "No need. There's only one guest, and they said they are leaving early. Later today, we're getting some new guests. You can have the day off."

She paused, staring off toward the far wall as if she were digesting my words before she glanced down. "Then I guess I'll see you tonight for your hot date."

It might have been my imagination, but I sensed a twinge of regret behind her mocking tone.

I narrowed my eyes, not happy that she'd signed me up for this, but intrigued as to why she was having a negative reaction to it. Perhaps, she wasn't happy that I was going?

Was that a possibility?

"Well, I have you to thank for that. Being my match-maker and all."

She scoffed. "I can also be your wedding planner if it should go that far."

I quirked an eyebrow. "Wedding planner?"

She nodded. "Yeah. I was pretty good at my job until I got—" Her eyes widened as she pinched her lips shut.

I was interested now. "Until you got...?"

She shook her head. "It doesn't matter now." Then she turned. "I'll be over to watch squirt for you at four? Five?" She peeked over her shoulder. "Weren't you saying something about being back at seven?"

I scoffed. "If I'm going on a date, I'll be out as long as she wants. It's been ages since I've had a night that's not full of pink pajamas and dinner in my hair." I pushed my hand through my hair and tipped my head back to study her.

Her gaze had fallen to my bicep, and her cheeks looked flushed. A smile played on my lips as I watched her stare for a moment before blinking and dragging her gaze to meet mine. I raised my eyebrows to let her know I saw.

She cleared her throat and broke her hold on my gaze. "Well, I hope for the sake of your daughter you are careful."

"Careful?"

Her eyes widened. "Careful." She fiddled with her purse strap. "Whomever you marry will be Belle's stepmom. I hope you're taking that responsibility seriously."

I wanted to laugh. This woman knew me. She grew up alongside me. We both knew the pain that came from parents who married casually and broke it off as soon as the marriage got hard. We both got emotionally attached to our stepparents just to have them walk away in the end.

"Please, Shelby. You feel like you need to tell me this?" She must not know me at all.

She stared at me. "Well, I just..." Her voice trailed off, and she stood there, looking like she wanted to say something but didn't know how to.

I was angry. I was hurt. I was frustrated that she'd forced me on this date in the first place. I slid a bit farther down the couch so I wouldn't startle Belle and stood. I crossed the space between us as I stared down at Shelby.

Her entire body tensed, but she didn't walk away. Instead, she stood there, staring up at me as if this was her form of defiance.

"What do you want from me?" I asked before I could stop myself. I was tired of feeling like this. If she hated me, I just wanted her to say it.

Her eyes widened, but she didn't look away. "I don't want anything from you," she whispered.

I wasn't buying it. "I think that's a lie. I think you want a lot of something. You're just not saying it."

She scoffed and dropped her gaze before bringing it up to the side and then eventually settling it on me. "I'm just thinking about Belle. She deserves the best life. And I don't want you thinking with..." She tipped her head down. "Other body parts than your brain when it comes to what her future looks like."

Anger rose up inside of me. "And why are you thinking about my other body parts?" I took a step closer to her. There was nothing I wanted more than to kiss her in this moment. To take her in my arms and watch that startled expression turn to pleasure from the things I could do to her.

My head was so full of thoughts—of feelings—that I feared what I might do if I let my guard slip any further.

"You should go," I said. I stepped back and pushed my hand through my hair before scrubbing my face. "I'm a grown man, Shelby. I don't need a babysitter. The most important person in my life is my daughter, and I would die before I let anything hurt her."

Shelby was watching me. I couldn't read her gaze, and the truth was, I was tired of trying to figure out what she wanted from me. We stood in silence. I could feel the tension in the air. She wanted to say something, but she wasn't.

And I wasn't sure I had the time or patience for this.

"You should go," I said again. I needed her to leave. I knew I couldn't have her like I wanted to, so for my sanity, I just needed her to walk out the door. To put distance between us, so I could once again heal from a broken heart caused by Shelby.

"Miles, I..." She took a step forward with her hand extended.

My muscles tightened involuntarily as I watched her hand stop just a few inches from my arm. I stared at it, willing her to close the gap. I wanted her to touch me. I wanted her to *voluntarily* touch me. Last night was amazing, but she'd been asleep.

I wanted her to touch me when she was awake.

Her eyes were wide, and she looked like a deer in headlights as she stood there, frozen. That's when I realized that I was being selfish. I was pushing Shelby further along this path than she was willing to go...or even wanted to go.

If I loved her, I'd let her take the time she needed to heal.

My entire body relaxed as I moved around to take her shoulders with both of my hands and lead her from the living room and through the kitchen. I pulled open the back door. "I understand what you're saying, Shelby," I said as I guided her out to the porch. "You don't have to worry about me and Laura. I don't see her that way. I'm just going because you set it up, remember?" I asked as I peered down at her.

She looked confused but managed a nod.

"Good. Now, go eat breakfast and take a shower. I'm going to take care of Belle. I will see you tonight." I let go of her shoulders and moved to walk back into the kitchen, but I lingered in the doorway, watching her try to process what had happened.

She shook her head and made her way down the stairs.

"Hey, Shelb?" I called after her.

She stopped and turned.

"Thanks for caring enough to fight me about this."

She raised her eyebrows but then nodded. "Of course." Then she started walking to the cottage, and I was left alone. I shut the door and leaned against it, tipping my head back.

What was wrong with me?

I'd made a promise to myself not to scare her away, and here I was, doing the exact opposite. If I didn't get myself in check, I was going to do something stupid, and Shelby would run again.

Leaving me alone with a broken heart once more.

SHELBY

SWEET TEA &
SOUTHERN GENTLEMAN

THE DAY SEEMED to drag on. After I barricaded myself in the cottage, I showered, ate, and then spent the morning on the internet trying to do everything but think about what had transpired between me and Miles.

There was a moment last night that I thought I felt Miles kiss me on the head and tell me he loved me, but I shook that off right away as a dream. A strange dream— one brought on by these feelings I was starting to have toward him. Ones that I didn't understand and really didn't want to process.

I was just in an emotional state, and I was clinging to the one person who was present and available. Plus, he was being so dang nice to me that his actions would confuse anyone.

It was only normal for me to feel this cloudy.

I spent the afternoon cooking myself some pasta and

watching Dr. Phil. Call me crazy, but I was determined to find an episode where he talked to estranged former step-siblings who were navigating how to deal with their new relationship after their grandmother died.

It was incredibly specific, and I tried not to be disappointed when I couldn't find an episode that addressed these issues. Instead, I got sucked into one about a mother who was keeping her husband's ashes in her bed.

By the time four o'clock rolled around, I'd done nothing but eat an entire bag of chips and watch five Dr. Phil episodes.

I brushed off the crumbs on my shirt and climbed out of the rocker I'd been camped out in all day. My phone chimed, and I hurried across the room to get it. Scrolling on social media and reading random celebrity news had drained the battery.

It was a text from Miles.

Miles: I need to leave in ten minutes. Does that work?

I shot back a thumbs-up emoji and hurried into my room to change out of my sweats and food-covered shirt. After running a brush through my hair and applying a bit of mascara and lip gloss, I stared at my reflection as the memory of Miles standing so close to me flooded my mind.

Had it meant something?

I shook my head. Of course, it didn't. I was being ridiculous to think that.

As I slipped on my flip-flops, my phone chimed again.

I hurried to grab it only to find that it was a message from Abigail.

Abigail: What are you doing tonight? Wanna hang out?

I paused and shot off a quick text before I opened the door and headed toward the inn.

Me: Can't. Watching Belle, Miles's daughter, tonight. Tomorrow?

She responded with a thumbs-up, and I slipped my phone into my back pocket as I hurried up the stairs and through the back door.

Miles was in the kitchen, unbuttoning the cuffs of his button-down shirt while Belle was in her high chair, eating a banana. When she saw me, her smile lit up her face. I grinned at her as I crossed the room and gave her a quick kiss on the cheek. "Are we going to hang out tonight?"

She giggled, but her mouth was so full of banana that no words could come out.

"Thanks for coming over."

Miles's voice drew my attention. I straightened, hating that these ridiculous butterflies were back. "Yeah, well, like you said earlier, this date was my doing. I need to see it through."

Miles was studying me as he rolled the sleeves of his blue button-up shirt to mid-forearm. Then he shrugged. "Still, I'm glad you are here." He grinned when his gaze slipped to Belle. "And she is too."

I tousled her hair, making sure not to pull any out of

the pigtails that Miles had done. Then I turned my attention back to Miles, who was tucking in his shirt. My cheeks warmed as I watched him.

He caught me watching, and I quickly dropped my gaze. "So, what are you guys going to do?"

"I don't know."

His response surprised me, and I brought my gaze over to study him. "What?"

He was fastening his belt. "I figured we'd get some food at the diner and then bring it to the beach to eat." He shrugged. "Or eat it there. I don't really know."

Jealousy rose up inside of me. He wanted to bring her to the beach? Those feelings startled me. Why was that affecting me like this? Not wanting him to notice, I shrugged, desperate to keep them from doing anything too romantic. "Staying at the restaurant sounds nice. You know, less sand."

He was studying me now. I hated how blue his eyes were. Or the way he'd styled his hair like he actually cared what Laura thought about him. I hated that his shoulders were broad and that I knew what kind of physique he had under that shirt.

I hated that I didn't want him to go. And my biggest fear was that he was going to fall in love with Laura before I could figure out why I hated all of these things.

His expression softened as if he could read my thoughts. I watched him take a few steps forward as he reached out his hand. "I don't have to go..." His voice drifted off, but he didn't look away. "If you want me to stay."

I swallowed. The words, "Please, stay," clung to my throat. I feared what those words would mean, so I just shrugged, glanced down at Belle, and patted her arm.

From the corner of my eye, I could see Miles staring at me. I cleared my throat and turned to give him a smile. "I'll —we'll be just fine," I said.

He didn't look like he believed me, but if that was the case, he didn't say anything. Instead, he just nodded and turned to the counter where his wallet was sitting. "You have my number. Call me if her temperature spikes again."

I nodded. "Got it. I can do that."

He glanced at his phone for a second before his thumb began to move as if he were texting someone. Was it wrong that I wanted to know who it was? I wanted to know if it was Laura and what he was saying to her.

Was he calling it off?

I shook my head and dropped my gaze to Belle. Of course, he wasn't calling it off. Why would he do that? I knew Miles, and he was a man of his word. He wouldn't say he would take Laura out just to call it off minutes before he had to leave to pick her up.

He slipped his phone into his pocket and crossed the room to stand next to us. My body warmed as he stood there. The smell of his cologne filled my nose and messed with my head. Suddenly, my heart was pounding, and all I wanted was for him to wrap me in his arms and pull me close.

I wanted him to touch me.

"Have you decided?" I asked, moving to stand on the other side of Belle's highchair to get away from him.

Miles had crouched down to smile at Belle, so he glanced up at me and held my gaze for a moment. "Decided what?" There was a depth to his voice that made me wonder what that was about.

"About the restaurant or the beach?"

He looked confused for a moment then he nodded as he stood up. "I think we're just going to hang out at the restaurant. I want to make sure I have cell service, and if we wander too far down the beach, I might lose it."

"You don't trust me?" I asked, feeling hurt and relieved at the same time. It was a strange sensation.

"What?"

"With Belle. Is that why you want to stay within cell-phone range?"

He frowned. "Are you saying that I should take Laura to the beach?"

I scoffed and shook my head. I didn't know what I was saying. Words were just spilling from my lips unchecked, and I couldn't pull them back. "I'm not saying that."

Miles crossed his arms. "So, I shouldn't?"

I studied him for a moment before I dropped my gaze and shrugged. "I think you should do what you want to do. Belle will be fine with me."

Suddenly, his shoes came into view, and his hands wrapped around my upper arms.

"Shelby?"'

I knew he wanted me to look at him. I could feel his stare even though I couldn't see it. "What, Miles?" I choked out.

He pulled me in until I crashed into his chest and his arms wrapped around me. His hand went to my head, and he held me against his shoulder. He was warm. His shirt was soft. And the smell of his cologne mixed with *him* swarmed all my senses until I let go of my fear and wrapped my arms around him.

A sob escaped my lips as he held me. "I'm sorry," I whispered.

He pulled back. "For what?"

I sniffled as I brought my hand up to wipe at his tear-stained shirt. "I ruined your clothes for your date."

He glanced down and chuckled. "That? It's fine. Belle's done worse."

I laughed, and we both glanced over at Belle. Miles was the first to look back at me. I could see him studying me.

"I'm sorry," he said, his voice deep and filled with emotion.

I finally gathered my courage to look back at him. "For what?"

"I should have gone after you. I should have been

there that night. I was..." A pained expression passed over his face, and I backed away.

I didn't want to talk about that night. I didn't want him to say he was sorry. The memories filled my head, and my entire body went numb. "Please, don't." Why did he bring that up? We were finally coming closer together as friends, and then he had to say that.

I shook my head as I turned, biting my lip as I forced my emotions to calm.

"Shelby, I'm—"

"Shouldn't you go? Laura is probably waiting for you." I offered him a weak smile.

He studied me, and I could tell that he didn't believe my words at all. Thankfully, he didn't push me. Instead, he nodded, gave Belle a kiss on the cheek, and glanced at me as he passed by. I didn't say anything until he was gone, and then I let out the breath I didn't know I'd been holding.

"What do you want to do, princess?" I asked as I made my way over to her high chair and squatted down so I could see her. She just giggled, placed both hands on my cheeks, and squished them together until my lips puffed out.

We spent the night playing with Play-Doh and the kitchen toys until she grew bored. We went into her room and played with her dolls. When her eyes grew weary, I changed her into her pajamas, and we made our way out into the living room for a princess movie.

I snuggled with her on the couch. Her eyes were wide as she watched the princess dancing around on the screen. I took out my phone and scrolled through my messages. There wasn't anything from Miles.

I don't know why that frustrated me. It was 7:30 and he still wasn't back. Was he enjoying himself? Was Laura that interesting of a person to talk to?

Was he going to kiss her when he dropped her off?

Thirty minutes later, Belle nodded off. She'd been snuggling on my chest, so I rested my hand on her back and changed the channel with my other hand. I finally settled on a cooking show. My eyes felt heavy, but there was no way I was going to miss Miles coming home. I needed to know how his date went.

Suddenly, the feeling of two arms sliding underneath my back and knees startled me awake. The room was dark except for the low glow of the TV. Miles was staring down at me when my eyes whipped open.

"What are you doing?" I asked.

He hoisted me up, pulling me close to his chest. "You fell asleep," he said.

I held onto Belle, terrified that he was going to drop us. "I can walk."

He shook his head. "I know my daughter. She doesn't like to be moved too much. So..." He paused as he glared down at me. "You hold her, and I'll hold you. It's time for bed."

I knew I should fight him. Being wrapped up in his

arms like this, having him care for me, wasn't good for the confusing feelings in my chest, but the protest never came.

Instead, I just let him carry me through the living room, the kitchen, and into Belle's room. He gently set me down on my feet in front of her crib, then he lowered the crib railing and I was able to slide her onto the mattress with little to no jostling.

She squirmed for a moment before she snuggled into the mattress. Miles draped her blanket over her, raised the railing, and suddenly, he was standing next to me.

His hand remained on the crib, but his body was centimeters from mine. "Thank you for that," he said, his voice low and his gaze so intense it took my breath away.

"For what?" I knew I should look away, but I couldn't. My gaze drifted down to his lips before I forced it back up.

That was a mistake. The look in his eyes intensified as he moved closer to me. "For taking care of my daughter. I appreciate it."

My mouth went dry. His chest was practically pressed against mine as he towered over me. "Of course. I love that little girl," I whispered.

He studied me for a moment before he tipped his head back and let out a low, guttural growl. Something inside of me broke, and all I wanted was to feel his lips on mine.

"Don't say that to me," he said, staring at me.

"What?" I whispered. I knew I needed to get out of here. If I didn't, I might do something that I would regret in the light of tomorrow.

"Tell me that you love my daughter. Hold her like she's your own." His fingers were on my exposed arms, tracing lines as he dragged them up and down, leaving goosebumps in their wake.

"Miles, I..." I knew I should say I didn't want this, but the truth was, I didn't know what I wanted. I'd felt so dead inside for so long that I'd doubted I would ever feel again. But having Miles standing here, touching me...seeing me. I finally felt alive.

I wasn't ready to give that up.

But as fast as it started, it stopped. Suddenly, Miles pulled his hand away from my arm and took a few giant steps back. He pushed his hands through his hair and dragged them both down his face.

"I'm sorry. I shouldn't have done that," he said, his voice muffled behind his hands.

I wrapped my arms around my chest. My heart felt like it was breaking, which made no sense. I didn't love Miles. He wasn't that kind of guy to me. He was my ex-stepbrother and one of the reasons my heart was in shambles. Why had I almost kissed him?

It was hormones and the fact that it had been so long since I'd been touched by a man that I was desperate to feel it again. I was desperate not to hurt.

"It's okay," I said, shaking off his reaction and words. "You're a little tipsy. Happens to the best of us." I straightened. "We got a little carried away. We're adults."

He was in the shadows of Belle's room now, staring at

me. I couldn't quite read his expression, and I wasn't sure if I wanted to. The moon cast its faint light into the room, barely lighting up his features.

When he didn't speak, I gave him a weak smile and turned toward the door. "I should go. I'm tired, and you've had a long night." I wanted to ask him. I wanted to know if he had fun with Laura, but I couldn't bring myself to say the words.

The last thing I wanted to hear was that he'd had a fabulous time and hadn't wanted to come home. I was strong enough to walk away from him, but for some reason, I wasn't strong enough to hear those words.

Just as I cleared the door, Miles's voice stopped me.

"Shelby?"

Shivers ran down my body from the sound of my name on his tongue. Suddenly, I was thinking about his lips and what they might feel like pressed to mine. Or pressed to my skin. My heart pounded as I closed my eyes, hating and loving the desire that was pumping through my body with each second that passed.

"Yeah?" I asked, flicking my response over my shoulder.

Silence.

My ears strained in case I'd missed something. I heard nothing but the soft breathing of Belle in her bed.

"Good night," he finally said, his deep voice warming me all over.

I glanced over my shoulder even though I knew I

shouldn't. His gaze was fixed on me, the light reflecting off his eyes. Heat burned through me. "You, too," I said, trying to ignore the fact that his gaze drifted down to my mouth as I spoke.

Not knowing what I would do if I stayed longer, I folded my arms and hurried out of the inn. The air was cooler when I stepped out onto the porch and closed the back door behind me. I ducked my head and crossed the yard and slipped into the cottage.

Once I was safely behind the door, I leaned against it, tipped my head back, and took in a deep breath.

What had that been?

Did I want...Miles?

I let that question linger in my mind before I shook it out and pushed off the door. I needed a hot shower and a good night's sleep. Tomorrow, I would think differently. Tomorrow, I wouldn't feel so confused.

Tomorrow, I wouldn't want to feel the hands of the man I thought I knew, roaming across my body.

SWEET TEA &
SOUTHERN GENTLEMAN

SCRATCHING.

I sat up in bed in the dead of night, my heart pounding
as I heard the same sound that had woken me all week.
Scratching at the front door.

I'd just fallen asleep after my very confusing interaction with Miles in Belle's bedroom, and my head was
swimming from thoughts of him and what could possibly
be at my front door. I swallowed my fear as I pulled the
covers from my body and slipped my feet onto the floor. I
straightened my pajama top and shuffled through the
bedroom to the living room and over to the front door.

Flashbacks of being attacked by a raccoon at the door
when I was a kid raced through my mind. I thought after
all these years I would be stronger...

I wasn't.

My hands shook as I tried to angle my head enough so I could see through the front window to the door.

Nothing. I couldn't see anything.

The noise stopped, and I slowly let out my breath, hoping that it wouldn't hear me and come back. I closed my eyes and willed my pounding heart to stop. Then I tiptoed back to the bedroom and crawled under the covers.

There was nothing there, and I was fine.

But, just in case, I pulled the covers over my head and lay there like a scared child. There was something about this place that made me feel small again.

I closed my eyes and hummed the lullaby my grandmother would sing to me when I got scared. I hated that it still brought me comfort after all of these years—but I was so confused by Miles and my feelings for him that I needed to pull out the big guns to calm my mind.

Scratching.

I muffled my scream as my body immediately tensed. I shot my hand out from beneath the blankets and grabbed my phone. I needed someone else to witness this. Miles still hadn't installed the camera like he said he was going to. So, I was left thinking that I was going crazy and hearing things.

Miles picked up on the third ring. "Shelby?"

"Miles?"

He cleared his throat. "Do you—"

"There's something scratching on my door." I closed my eyes, hating that I felt this weak.

"What?"

"My door. The front door. There's something there, and I can't—" It suddenly dawned on me what I was doing, and I pulled the phone from my cheek and pressed the red end-call button. I shook my head as I buried my phone deep in my pillows and flopped down.

What had I been thinking? I didn't want Miles to come here. The last thing I needed was for him to rescue me. I was confused enough about the man. I shouldn't have him in my space when I wasn't sure if I wanted to push him away or pull him in for a kiss. Why was I asking him to confuse me more?

"That was stupid, and we aren't going to do stupid things anymore," I murmured to myself as I flipped to my side and felt the comforter settle around me.

I closed my eyes and steadied my breathing. As long as I was in here, whatever it was out there couldn't hurt me.

The sound of the front door slamming open startled me. Fearing the worst—that a Sasquatch finally figured out how to open the door—I peeked out over my comforter only to see Miles standing in the doorway of my room, his eyes wild.

He scanned the room, and as soon as he saw me in bed, he headed toward me. I wanted to protest, but I was too distracted by his bare chest. His pajama bottoms were slung low on his hips. My stomach lightened when I saw he'd clipped Belle's baby monitor to his pocket.

Suddenly, the blankets were being pulled off, and Miles's arms slid under me.

"What are you—"

"I can't protect you and my daughter in separate houses. So, for tonight, you're coming with me," he growled as he pulled me against his chest.

Every atom in my body was zinging from the feeling of my bare skin against his. His heart was pounding, and I could feel his tense muscles as he kept me close, walking through the cottage, across the porch, and over to the inn.

I wrapped my arms around his neck as he walked. There was a moment there when I saw him glance down at me, but I didn't have the strength to meet his gaze. I needed to focus on where he was taking me, not the fact that his heart was pounding as hard as mine.

He didn't set me down as he reached his hand out and found the door handle. He didn't stop once we got into the kitchen. He didn't stop until he was standing next to his bed, holding me over it.

"Miles," I whispered, not sure I was going to survive the night if I slept next to him.

"Shelby," his voice was gruff as he gently laid me down. "Please. Let me take care of you for the night." He knelt down in front of me, his head dipped down as if he were carrying the weight of something unimaginable on his shoulders. When he glanced up, there was a pain in his gaze that took my breath away. "I failed you before, and I can't..." His voice broke, and suddenly, realization dawned on me.

"Miles, I—"

"Don't. I'm not asking you to talk about it. I just want you here, where I can see you. Where I can take care of you." His gaze dropped to my hands grasped together on my lap. I couldn't tell if he was just looking or if he wanted to grab them.

I wasn't sure what I wanted him to do.

"Will you do that for me?" He slowly raised his gaze back to meet mine.

Not able to take the intensity of his stare, I glanced around the room. "Are you sleeping in the bed with me?" I asked, not sure which answer I wanted to hear.

His eyebrows rose. "Do you want me to?"

I chewed my lip and watched as his gaze drifted down to my mouth before rising back up to my eyes. I should have said no. I needed him to leave...but I didn't want him to.

"Yes," I finally whispered.

He swallowed, every muscle in his jaw shifting. He stared at me for a moment before he nodded and stood. "Okay."

He rounded the bed while I scooted to the top and pulled the comforter out from under me. Miles stood next to the mattress and glanced around as if he wasn't sure what he was going to do. I pulled the comforter back, exposing the sheet.

"Come on," I said.

His gaze moved to mine and then he obeyed. I felt the mattress shift under his weight as he settled next to me. He had his arm bent and resting under his head as he lay there on his back.

"I promise you'll be safe here," he said. All I could see was his profile.

"I know," I whispered. There weren't a lot of things that I knew, but in this moment, I knew that Miles would protect me.

I'd never thought this man could love a little girl like he loved Belle. She was his world, and he carried his daughter's monitor around like it was his lifeline. He'd changed.

His body stiffened at my words. Then he slowly tipped his head until he was staring at me. I could see that he wanted to say something; I just wasn't sure if I was strong enough to hear it.

I dropped my gaze to the mattress as I lay there on my side, drawing circles on the sheet. I wasn't ready. I wasn't ready for whatever he had to say.

"I'll install a camera tomorrow," he said.

"Thanks." I brought my hands up under my chin as I snuggled deeper into the pillow tucked under my head. "I'm exhausted," I said as I closed my eyes.

"Go to sleep," he said. I didn't mind the commanding tone he took as my entire body relaxed.

Whatever was going on between us could be sorted

out tomorrow. For tonight, I was going to lie here and revel in the fact that, for the first time in a long time, I wasn't alone.

And it felt amazing.

THE SMELL of bacon and maple syrup wafted into the room, waking me. I shifted against the mattress, stretching out my hand to feel for Miles. And then I felt stupid when I came up empty-handed. Who did I think was cooking if Miles was still in bed?

And then it hit me. I'd looked for him. Which meant I wanted him to be here. With me. In bed.

I closed my eyes and brought my hand in close to my heart as I curled around my stomach. What was happening? Why was I feeling these things? This was Miles. He wasn't my prince charming or my knight in shining armor. He was confusing me, that was all.

"Belle." Miles's whisper pricked against my ears.

I squinted as I watched him tiptoe around the bed with a tray in his hands. Belle must be with him because his gaze wasn't on me but on something on the other side of the room. And from the grimace on his face, he wasn't too happy with what she was doing.

Not wanting to make this awkward, I stretched and moved to sit up. Miles eyes widened as he stood next to the bed.

"You're up."

I nodded and used both of my hands to push myself up into a sitting position. "Yeah. I just woke up a few minutes ago." From where I was sitting, I could see that Belle had pulled open one of the dresser drawers and was now pulling out Miles's boxers.

"Belle," he said again, this time louder. I giggled at his reddening cheeks.

"Hang on," he said as he set the tray down on my legs and hurried over to scoop her up. After he tucked his boxers back into the drawer, he blew a raspberry into her neck, slipped his arm under her bum, and held her to his chest.

"I made bacon and French toast..." He paused as if he suddenly realized he'd let out a secret.

"My favorite?" I asked, my chest swelling to the point where it felt like it was going to burst.

He stared at the food before he slowly brought his gaze over to meet mine. "Your favorite." There was so much emotion in his voice that it lowered a whole octave.

"Thanks," I said, not sure what I was supposed to say to that.

He studied me for a moment before Belle brought her little chubby hands up to his cheeks and pressed on them. That broke his concentration as he glanced down at her.

"You eat while I go feed this monster," he said as he kissed her cheeks and she giggled.

"Okay," I said, pulling the tray further up onto my lap.

He stared at the comforter before he nodded and moved to leave the room, pausing at the door for a moment and then disappearing down the hallway.

I stared at the empty space he'd left behind, wondering if he was going to come back. And then I started wondering if I wanted him to come back.

Shaking that thought from my mind, I grabbed the little pitcher of syrup and drizzled it all over the French toast.

If I didn't have feelings for Miles before, I certainly did after I inhaled that breakfast. My tastebuds were tingling, and my stomach felt satisfied as I set down my utensils and moved the tray off my lap. Just as my feet touched the ground, Miles came into the room as if he'd been waiting in the hallway.

"You done?" he asked.

I nodded and watched him close the space between us. When he leaned forward to grab the tray, I suddenly realized how close he was to me. His chest brushed my shoulder, and he must have realized it as well because he glanced over at me and completely froze.

I held his gaze, scared of what I might find there but also intrigued by the way his look made me feel. It was like the taste of French toast and the feeling of home were all wrapped up in his gaze.

"Did you like it?" he asked, not moving to pull away.

"What?" I asked. My gaze drifted slowly down to his lips before I forced it back up.

He saw. And he wasn't shy about seeing. Heat burned in his gaze as he leaned half an inch closer to me. "The breakfast," he said. It was so quiet and low that it sounded more like a rumble in his chest.

"Yes," I whispered, moving the same distance toward him. What would it feel like to kiss him? To feel his strong arms wrap around me. To feel them pull me closer until I wasn't sure where my body ended and his began.

He grinned. "I'm happy."

"You are?"

He nodded.

"Hey, Miles?" Mrs. Porter's voice snapped us both from our trance. Suddenly, he was standing in front of me with the tray wrapped tightly in his hands. "Yeah?" he asked, tipping his face toward the door but not making any indication that he was going to move.

"Just wanted to let you know that I was here," she said, her voice growing closer.

Panic filled my chest as I began to slide off the bed. Miles set the tray down and wrapped his hands on my upper arms, pulling me up. Then I was against his chest as he dropped his arm around my shoulders and guided me toward his closet doors.

Once I was inside, he pressed his forefinger to his lips and shut the doors.

"Oh, here you are," Mrs. Porter's voice was in the bedroom now.

The doors weren't see-through, but I could see shadows. "Here I am," Miles said as he turned to face her.

"I thought I heard someone in here..." Mrs. Porter's shadow had appeared. "Did you make yourself breakfast in bed?"

Miles crossed the room and picked up the tray. "Yep. It's what I like to call a little R&R," he said as he moved behind Mrs. Porter and started to walk forward, effectively guiding her shadow out of the room.

"R&R?"

"Yeah, it's extremely important..." Miles's voice faded.

I let out my breath. That had been close. Too close. I winced and shook my head. I needed to be more careful. The last thing I needed was a rumor going around Harmony that I was dating Miles. The scandal. The things people would say. It would feed the rumor mill for far too long. I wasn't even sure what was going on between us, and the last thing I needed was for others to confuse me.

Miles returned five minutes later with an exasperated look on his face. Whatever had happened between us last night and this morning, I forced it into the lockbox in my mind. That's where it needed to stay.

He pressed his finger to his lips and nodded toward the front of the inn. I tiptoed down the hall, bypassed the kitchen where I could hear Mrs. Porter singing to Belle, and escaped out the front door.

Luckily, no guests saw me and my walk of shame as I

padded across the porch and down to the dewy grass. I made it back to my cottage, cursed the stupid front door and whatever had been scratching at it, and then hurried inside. I shut the door behind me and let out my breath.

That had been...

Unexpected.

20

ABIGAIL

SWEET TEA &
SOUTHERN GENTLEMAN

I WOKE up Friday morning in a good mood. I'd had dinner at Anders's place, and after we ate, we snuggled on the couch, which led to a very memorable make out session.

I finally dragged myself into the apartment at ten only to find Sabrina lying on the couch with Samuel screaming in his crib. I hurried her off to bed and spent the night alternating between rocking Samuel and trying to sleep on the rocking chair so as not to disturb him.

Even though I was exhausted, the thrill I felt from my night with Anders had my heart pounding. He really was perfect.

I was readying some cookie dough when my phone rang. I rinsed my hands and picked it up. Dad was calling.

"Hey," I said as I slipped my phone between my

shoulder and cheek. I washed my hands again and returned to the dough.

"Hey, Abi."

I smiled at my dad's term of endearment for me. We'd had a rocky relationship ever since Mom died and he went AWOL. But after his return last year and some meddling from Penny—his new wife—we were on the mend.

"Hey, Dad."

He paused. "I tried calling Sabrina."

I stopped what I was doing and glanced toward the front windows. I wasn't surprised that she didn't answer, but a small flicker of worry simmered in my gut that she would have so quickly gotten distracted. She seemed chipper this morning, so I figured today was going to be a good day.

"Huh. She was awake when I left."

"Maybe she's changing Samuel?"

"Probably."

"Well, Penny wanted me to call and check up on you two."

I smiled. Typical Dad. He didn't want to intrude even though I told him numerous times that him calling me was never intruding. "Thanks."

"Tell her that we want to come out next month." I could hear Penny's voice in the background.

"Penny wants me to tell you that we're planning a trip out there."

"You are? When?"

Dad's muffled voice asked, "When?" before I heard Penny say, "Here, let me do it. Abigail?"

"Hey, Penny."

"I was hoping to get Jackson to your bookstore for a signing next month. What do you think about that?"

"Jackson here? At my store?"

"Yes."

"That's..." My heart surged at her words. I knew Penny wasn't one for sap, but for the first time in a long time, I felt happy. I had Anders, a mother figure, and my dad in my life. If I had my sister back, my life would be perfect.

"That would be great," I finally said as I shook off my emotions and focused on the present.

"Awesome. We'll see you then."

"Sounds good."

We said our goodbyes, and I let my phone slip from my shoulder and land on the dish towel on the counter next to me. I tried to silence the fear in my mind that Sabrina wasn't answering her phone as I scooped dough onto the cookie sheets. My mind felt like quicksand.

I heard knocking at the front door. I glanced up to see Anders standing in front of the window. He gave me a small wave. I smiled and yelled, "Hang on."

After washing my hands, I grabbed the towel as I made my way to the door and unlocked it. As soon as I pulled the door open, Anders had his hands on my waist and pressed his lips to mine.

He groaned when he pulled back. "You taste like sugar," he said before he went in for another kiss.

I giggled against his lips. "That's what happens when you date a cafe owner."

He pulled back but kept his hands planted firmly on my hips. "I'm one lucky guy," he said with a wink and then nuzzled his face into my neck and trailed kisses to my ear. "I missed you when you left last night," he said against my skin.

"I know," I said as I pulled away. Anders wasn't too happy that I'd left, but Sabrina needed me home, and I wasn't quite ready to bring our romantic relationship to the next level. We were still getting to know each other, and I didn't feel like I was ready for what Anders so obviously wanted.

"Are you two done?"

A deep voice startled me, and I glanced over Anders' shoulder to see Bash standing there. He wasn't wearing black this time. Instead, he had on a blue t-shirt and jeans. He had his hands shoved into his front pockets, and he looked completely uncomfortable. Well, from the little I could see through the hair draped across his face.

"Killjoy," Anders complained in my ear before he pulled back.

I swatted Anders with the towel and allowed my gaze to drift over to Bash, who had yet to meet my gaze. "What are you two doing here?" I asked.

"I have to go out of town for work, and Bash got tired

of hearing me rave about your food. He said he had to come down here with me."

"I did not." Bash glared at Anders

Anders raised his hands and let out a loud laugh. "Just kidding. I told him I'd buy him breakfast if he actually left the apartment today."

"He leaves the apartment," I said before I could stop myself.

Anders and Bash turned to look at me as heat pricked the back of my neck. I swallowed and shrugged. "I mean, wouldn't he be pale if he never got sun?"

Anders stepped back and ran his gaze over Bash. "Now that Abigail mentions it, you are looking tanner." He leaned closer. "Do you have a secret life that I don't know about?"

Bash squinted and moved to turn away. "I'm going back home—"

"Geez, man. It's a joke. I'll buy you breakfast," Anders said as he reached out and grabbed Bash's arm.

Bash paused before he turned back around. Not sure what was going on between the two of them, I swung the towel over my shoulder and nodded toward the kitchen. "I'll get some food cooking then."

Anders and Bash talked while I made up some sausage and egg croissants. Even if it was awkward to have Bash here, it was nice to cook and listen to the two of them talk and laugh. Well, Anders talk and laugh. Bash just sat there; his entire body was stiff as he studied his friend.

I dished up their food, and the cafe was silent as they ate. I returned to cookie making. When they were done, Anders let out a moan of pleasure.

"You sure do know how to tickle a man's tastebuds, Abi," he said as he pushed his plate to the side and leaned over the counter. He grabbed my shirt and pulled me to him, smashing his lips to mine.

I'd been too stunned to brace myself, and in his efforts, he ended up knocking the scoop from my hand. If he noticed, he didn't move to correct his mistake. Instead, he took the kiss a little too far, trying to shove his tongue in my mouth.

I didn't respond, and thankfully, he didn't push it further. His phone rang, so he pulled back and pressed his lips to my cheek before letting me go. I stood there with a now empty hand trying to figure out what the heck just happened.

Anders slipped his phone into his pocket as he declared he was heading out. After a loud smack on Bash's shoulder, he blew me a kiss and left.

I blinked a few times, trying to process the events, before I saw movement next to me and realized that Bash was still here. But he was no longer sitting at the counter. He'd stood as he reached across the counter and grabbed Anders' discarded plate.

"Sorry about that," he said as he stacked the plates, moved around the counter, and lingered on the outskirts of the kitchen as if he wasn't sure if it was okay for him to come in.

I shook my head to wake up and then glanced over at him. "Did you say sorry?" Had my ears deceived me?

He met my gaze for a moment before shifting it to the plates in his hands. "I was just apologizing for Anders's behavior?"

"Behavior?"

Bash must have given up waiting on me to invite him in because he stepped across the threshold and over to the sink. I was leaning against the counter, watching him, as I tried to process what was happening.

"Anders can be oblivious to the world sometimes," he said as he moved over to me.

My entire body tensed, but he didn't touch me. Instead, he crouched down and picked up the fallen cookie scoop.

"Do you do this a lot?"

Bash had returned to the sink and was now filling it with hot, soapy water. "Do what?"

"Apologize for your friend." I waved my hand at the dishes. "Clean up his mistakes."

Bash's shoulders tightened as if my words struck a chord. I paused, wondering what that was about and if I even had any reason to prod further.

"Listen, Anders likes you. I just want to make sure you realize what you are getting into." He dunked the first dish into the water and started wiping it down.

"Getting myself into..." Now I was confused. Who was this guy?

"You know what? Never mind. I should have never said anything." He rinsed the plate and then stood there with it dripping into the sink.

Not wanting to just stand there, I took it from him and grabbed the dish towel on my shoulder and started drying it off. "Why are you doing this?" I asked before I could stop myself.

He stopped and then glanced over his shoulder. He'd returned to the sink and was washing the second plate. "Doing what?"

I had so many questions running through my mind, and I wasn't sure how I was going to get any of them out. "What are you doing in Harmony? You are obviously not from here, and Anders is here for a job." I narrowed my eyes at him. "What's your story?"

He paused, holding my gaze before dropping his focus back to the sink. "Do I have to have a story?"

"Everyone has a story."

He sighed, his shoulders dropping. "Mine's not interesting. Therefore, it doesn't deserve repeating." He turned on the faucet and rinsed the plate.

I stepped up and took it from him, my fingers brushing his in the process. My whole body froze, and it seemed that Bash had the same reaction as his gaze drifted over to me. We stood there in silence as our gaze met.

Then he pulled his hand back at the same time I did,

and the plate went crashing to the ground, breaking into shards before either of us could catch it. Suddenly, Bash cupped his ears and bent forward as if the sound had triggered something in him.

"Bash?" I leaned forward and rested my hand on his shoulder.

His hand was on mine before I even knew what was happening. Then he was scooping me up, pulling me tight to his chest. There was a panic in his gaze that caused me to pinch my lips shut as he took a wide step over the plate and carried me around the cafe counter and hid me behind it.

I was now on the ground, and he was crouching in front of me, his gaze raking over my face and then the rest of my body.

"Are you hurt?" he asked. The panic in his voice was palpable.

"I'm fine," I said as I stretched out my hands so he could see that I hadn't been cut.

He looked over me, and when he glanced back at me, I could see understanding pass through his eyes. He stumbled backward and straightened as he pushed his hands through his hair, exposing a long, dark scar down the left side of his face. I only saw it for a second before his hair fell back over his face.

"I should—I should go," he muttered as he turned and hurried to the front door.

Before I could even get a word out, he was outside and disappearing around the corner of the building.

I sat under the counter for a moment, trying to get my bearings. Whatever that had been was strange. But as much as I wanted to be uninterested in Bash—the truth was the exact opposite. I needed to know who Bash was and what the heck he was doing here.

I finally gathered my wits about me and made my way back to the kitchen to clean up the broken plate.

I was pulling cookies from the oven when my phone chimed. I set the hot cookie sheet down on the counter and pulled off my oven mitt so I could check it.

It was a text from Shelby.

Shelby: I need alcohol. Tonight? The pub?

I needed that as well, so I sent a thumbs-up followed by "8 p.m."

I needed to check on Sabrina and Samuel. Then I was going to the pub for a girls night where I was determined to drink away my confusion toward both Anders and Bash.

21

SHELBY

SWEET TEA &
SOUTHERN GENTLEMAN

I SPENT the day avoiding any long conversations with Miles. After I snuck back to the cottage, I showered, dressed, and wasted time on social media until Miles texted me to see if I could watch Belle for a few hours, so he could get rooms ready for guests.

I agreed, asking if she could come over here instead of me watching her at the inn. When he brought her over, I quickly took her from his arms and hurried into the cottage before he could say anything. We played on the living room floor until she got cranky, and then I made her some food before taking her outside for a small picnic.

She was snoozing on the couch when Miles came to pick her up late in the afternoon. His eyebrows rose when he saw her. I was on the couch with my arm slung across the back, listening to some soft music. My heart pounded as I took him in. His hair was damp, and for a stupid split second, I wondered what it would feel like to run my fingers through it.

Hating that I couldn't stop thinking about Miles like that, I shook my head and gave him a weak smile.

"She's worn out," I said as I carefully got up so that I didn't disturb her.

"Clearly."

Worry flowed through me. "Was I not supposed to let her sleep?" I stepped toward Belle, but a hand stopped me. Somehow, Miles had closed the distance between us and wrapped his hand around my elbow.

"It's okay. If she needs to sleep, let her sleep." His voice was deep, and it sent ripples of pleasure through my body.

I expected him to let me go, but he didn't. Instead, we just stood in the living room, standing inches from each other, neither of us knowing what to do.

"Miles..." I whispered. I had no idea what I was going to say after that, but I needed to do something to break the tension that coated the room.

He pulled his hand away and took a step back. "I don't think she noticed."

Confused, I turned to look at him. "What?"

He waved toward the inn before he shrugged. "Miss Porter. I don't think she knows you were in my...bedroom this morning. I suspect if she knew, she would have said something to me about it. You're in the clear."

I parted my lips but only responded with a nod.

"So, you don't have to worry about the whole town wondering if we are..." He swallowed, and his pause caused me to look over at him. "Dating."

"That's good." My gaze made its way to his. His blue eyes were stormy as he stared at me. I could tell that he felt as confused as I did. "I'm going out with Abigail tonight, so I won't be around."

"Abigail?"

"She runs the bookstore-slash-cafe."

Recognition passed over his face as he nodded. "Right. Oh, Ralph dropped off your car. It's parked in the inn's parking lot. He texted me at noon. Apparently, I was wrong. It wasn't the oil. He was able to save it."

I clapped my hands. "Perfect."

Silence fell between us once more. Miles had his gaze trained on the ground before he looked up at me. I knew he wanted to say something. So much had transpired between us, and I wasn't sure what any of it meant—or if I was in a place to try to analyze any of it.

I wrapped my arms around my chest and offered him a small smile.

He seemed to understand that I was ready to be alone, because he didn't wait before he crossed the room and scooped up Belle. She let out a small moan and started to pull her head off his shoulder. He shushed her and brought his hand up to cradle her head.

She wiggled, and he gave me a weak smile as he

started heading to the front door. "I guess I'll talk to you tomorrow," he said over his shoulder.

I hurried to open the door, bringing myself inches from him. "Yeah," I said as I turned the handle and pulled.

He paused. "Just do me a favor."

"Sure."

He was staring at me now. "Just don't drink too much. And don't..."

I stood there, waiting for the rest of his words, but they didn't come. When I glanced up at him, I could see the turmoil in his gaze. "Don't?"

He blinked and then shook his head. "Never mind. Just enjoy yourself."

"Okay."

He stepped out onto the porch and didn't look back as he crossed the yard and disappeared into the inn. I hadn't meant to watch him the entire time, but there was a pathetic part of me that wished he would turn around and look at me. That he would finish his sentence, telling me that he didn't want me to go.

I was starting to realize that I had feelings for Miles. Deep, rooted feelings that I feared I would never get over if I was reading him wrong. I'd never imagined that I would want something with Miles—after all, I'd spent most of my life either thinking of him as a friend or hating him. But something had changed.

If I didn't find out how he felt, I was going to explode.

I spent the rest of the evening blaring music as I got ready. Abigail had texted to meet her at the pub at eight. At seven thirty, I slipped on my wedges and hurried out of the cottage. I was wearing a dark-blue dress that clung to my curves in all the right places.

I wasn't really going to the pub with the intention of picking anyone up. I just wanted to make sure if I ran into anyone from high school, I'd see appreciation in their gaze instead of pity.

Miles was outside on the deck when I rounded the inn in search of my car. I couldn't help but meet his gaze. His expression was hard to read as he stood there with his arms folded across his chest. I knew he was watching me and that thought burned my cheeks.

He watched as I unlocked my car and climbed inside. I tried not to sneak a peek at him from my rearview mirror, but my gaze slipped to it a few times as I drove away from the inn. And he was standing there, the entire time.

Once I couldn't see the inn anymore, I let out the breath I'd been holding and focused on the road. I was going to go insane if I kept obsessing about him. I pushed all the confusing thoughts from my mind as I headed toward Harmony Pub on the other side of town.

Dusk had settled around me as I pulled into one of the few remaining parking spots. I was climbing out of my car when I got a text from Abigail. I shut my door and glanced around to see her walking toward me.

She looked as confused as I felt, but when our gazes met, we both smiled.

As she neared, she wrapped me up in a hug. "You look amazing," she said as she stepped back.

"You too." She was wearing a white crop top and ripped shorts.

She linked arms with me. "You have no idea how much I needed this. Thanks for asking me out on a girls night."

I nodded as we started walking toward the pub. "I need this too."

She glanced over at me. "You do? What's going on?" Then she dropped her voice. "Miles?"

I shook my head. "I don't want to think tonight; I just wanted to dance and breathe."

Abigail nodded. "Me too."

The music in the pub was so loud, but I loved it. I could feel the reverberations in my chest. Abigail and I snagged a table as a couple was leaving. I slid onto a chair, and Abigail said she was heading to the bar. I wasn't sure if I wanted to drink. After all, every bad mistake I'd made involved alcohol, and the last thing I needed was to make another.

Abigail gave me a confused look but then shrugged and headed to the bar to order. I sat on the chair, drumming my fingers to the beat of the music, when suddenly, Laura was standing in front of me with the widest grin.

I almost didn't recognize her. Her cheeks were pink, and her hair was teased when she grabbed my arm.

"I can't thank you enough," she yelled to be heard over the music.

"What?" I leaned forward.

"Thank you."

I furrowed my brow. "For what?"

"For making Miles go out with me." She wiggled her eyebrows. "We had a *killer* time."

My stomach sank like a rock in my gut. "You did?"

She nodded, which sent her into a fit of giggles. "I'm pretty sure he's going to call me back." Then she leaned closer. "If you know what I mean." Her face contorted for a moment. "We had sex," she said so loud that the table next to us turned to look.

Even though the music was so loud it hurt my ears, I couldn't hear a thing. Not after what she just said to me. "What?"

She giggled once more and then half walked, half staggered away.

I sat there completely numb. Miles had slept with her and then come home and touched me? I shivered. My mouth felt dry and my head swam as I stared at the table in front of me like it held the answers I was seeking.

Why would he do that? I knew Miles. I knew he wasn't that kind of guy. At least, I thought I knew him.

"What's wrong?" Abigail asked when she got back to the table, holding a pint.

I slid off the chair and stood. "I'm getting a drink," I said as I shouldered my purse.

Five shots later, I was a mess. I was lying on the table, my stomach aching. No amount of alcohol was going to make me feel better. Abigail seemed just as miserable as I was. She was pushing some salt around on the table.

We looked like a pathetic party.

"I'm going to dance with someone." I pushed myself up and scanned the room. I didn't care who it was. As long as they distracted me from my thoughts and Miles, they were good enough. I zeroed in on an exotic looking man who had one elbow on the bar and was surveying the room.

He looked good enough.

When I got close, I grabbed his hand and yelled, "Dance with me."

"Ooh, I like a forceful girl. Name's Parker. What's yours?"

I shook my head. I didn't want small talk. I wanted Miles out of my head. "Just dance."

He didn't need any convincing. As soon as we were on the dance floor, his hands were on my waist. I wanted to dance away my feelings for Miles, but every time Parker touched me, I looked back hoping it was Miles, but only finding Parker's dark eyes and wide smile.

This wasn't fixing my broken heart.

"I'm tired," I yelled after the fourth song.

Parker nodded and kept his hand on my hip as I made

my way back to the table. I was so numb and broken, that I didn't care that he kept touching me. There was a part of me that hoped I'd enjoy his attention enough to forget Miles for one night.

But then Laura passed by my table, and suddenly I needed to text Miles. I needed him to know that I was desired by other men the same way I desired him.

"Who are you calling, baby?" Parker asked as he nuzzled my neck.

I shrugged him off. "I need to text Miles."

"Who's Miles?"

"It's her ex-stepbrother," Abigail yelled. She was sitting at the table, staring at her phone, as well.

"Yeah," I said as I opened my text messages and found Miles's name.

Me: Men want me, you know.

I hit send and set my phone down, screen up, in front of me.

The seconds that ticked by felt like hours. My heart pounded when my screen lit up.

Miles: Are you drunk?

I scoffed. Was he judging me?

Me: No.

And then I realized that he wasn't going to buy that.

Me: Maybe.

I set my phone back down, hoping my response came across as mysterious instead of neurotic like I feared it might. But the alcohol mixed with the music had my head pounding.

Miles: Where are you?

"Ha," I said as I picked up my phone. What did he care? The love of his life, Laura, was here. It shouldn't matter where I was.

Me: I'm fine. Parker's here.

I patted Parker's hand, but he was busy watching an exceptionally busty woman walk by. Bile rose up in my chest, and I swallowed it down. Parker wasn't boyfriend material. But I wasn't in any shape to be girlfriend material, so what did it matter?

Miles: Who's Parker?

I started to type out my answer, but Miles didn't give me enough time.

Miles: I'm coming to get you.

I scoffed and set my phone down. I doubted he would actually come, which was okay with me. I'd successfully bugged him, and that made me feel good. Especially with what Laura had said to me.

Two could play at this game.

Parker started to look bored. He kept asking me if we could dance, but I wasn't in the mood. Instead, I kept my arm draped over him, which seemed to satiate him enough to stay.

Abigail had her head down on her elbow as she rested on the table. We were a pathetic-looking group of people.

"Get up."

Miles's hard tone and deep voice startled me. I glanced up to see him standing right next to Parker, glaring at him.

"Miles?" I asked, wondering if I was dreaming or if he was really standing here.

"I said, get up."

Parker looked confused as well. "Hey, man," he said when Miles hooked his hand around his arm and lifted him off the seat. "Geez, I'm getting up." He stumbled to get his footing and yank his arm away from Miles.

"Stay away from her." Miles took a step forward and Parker threw up his hands.

"We're cool, dude. She's a hot mess anyway," he said as he walked away.

When Miles turned his gaze back to me, I could see the fire roaring inside of it.

"Get your purse. We're leaving."

I wanted to protest, but I didn't have the strength or fortitude. Instead, I just nodded and slid off the stool. Miles was rousting Abigail, and soon, he had his arms around both of us as he helped us to the door.

Laura came rushing over to him, and I almost puked on her, but Miles just brushed her off, telling her he didn't have time. I tried not to smile at the hurt look on her face as he half led, half carried the two of us out of the pub.

Abigail was awake enough to give him directions to her apartment, and he helped her inside. I called out the window that I would call her tomorrow before I collapsed against the seat and closed my eyes.

Miles climbed into the driver's seat and shut the door behind him. We drove in silence through town and out to the inn. I wanted to ask Miles so many questions, but I didn't know how to say any of them.

He turned off his headlights when he pulled into the parking lot, and he climbed out of his truck once he parked. I tried to leave with the same amount of speed, but I couldn't coordinate myself enough.

Miles pulled open the passenger door, unbuckled me, and lifted me out of my seat.

"Hey," I said, shifting to protest.

He just tightened his grip.

I wanted to fight, but there was something about being this close to him that soothed me. I felt my body relax. I was too tired to fight him. So, I just spent the entire time he carried me glaring at him. If he noticed, he didn't acknowledge it.

When we were in the kitchen, he set me down and stared at me for a moment before he turned and left. I could hear him talking to someone in the living room, thanking them for keeping an ear out for Belle. Silence fell around me, and I wondered if he'd gone to bed, forgetting all about me.

But seconds later, he appeared from the hallway that led to their bedrooms, a frustrated look on his face.

"What was that?" he asked as he crossed the kitchen and got down a glass.

"I don't know what you're talking about," I said, folding my arms across my chest in a sad attempt to protect myself.

Miles filled the glass with water. His gaze never left my face, which just left me feeling raw and vulnerable. He crossed the space between us and handed me the glass. I took it, hating that even though he looked frustrated with me, he was still trying to take care of me.

"Shelby, what are you doing?"

I took a drink. My anger and the coolness of the water was helping clear the clouds in my mind. I felt stupid and hurt. But most of all, I felt heart broken. Why didn't he mention that he and Laura had gotten so close? Why was he stringing me on like this?

"I was fine before you came in. Parker was right where I wanted him, and I was enjoying myself," I lied. I placed the bottom of the glass in my palm and wrapped my fingers up the side.

Miles was staring at me with an expression I couldn't read. "Really?" he finally asked.

"Really." I shrugged. "It's not a big deal. After all, it's not like you and I have anything going on." I scoffed, hating that the words clawed at my chest. Why did I want something different?

"We don't?"

I glanced up at him. Was he joking? I set the glass

down and took a step back. I needed some space to breathe. He was too close, and it was confusing me. "Yeah. We don't."

He swallowed, and I watched every muscle in his neck move. He was fighting something, and for some reason that angered me. He was the one who'd picked someone else over...whatever we had.

"I saw Laura at the pub."

His gaze flicked up to meet mine. "Yeah?"

I nodded. "She had some illuminating things to tell me."

He frowned. "Like what?"

I sighed and moved to the wall where the pictures of my childhood hung. I was so angry with Miles that it was crowding out the pain I usually felt when I stared at them. Right now, all I wanted was to stop hurting.

I chewed my bottom lip. "What are we doing, Miles? I feel like I've been an idiot ever since I walked back into this inn." I crossed my arms. "I should have never come back."

His hand was on my shoulder, and Miles spun me around. He stepped forward, pressing my back against the wall. He pressed his hands on either side of me, caging me in. He stared down at me, the fire in his gaze sparking a volcanic eruption in my stomach.

"If you hate me so much, just say the words," he growled as his gaze bored into mine.

I parted my lips a few times, trying to figure out the

words I wanted to say, but nothing was coming to me. Instead, I felt like a fish as I tried to gather my thoughts enough to sound coherent.

Miles noticed my lips, and when his gaze dropped to study my mouth, the desire to kiss him flooded every cell in my body. I wanted him. I wanted his lips on mine. His hands on my body. I wanted to feel every part of him.

But I was scared.

"Did you sleep with Laura?"

"What?" His gaze snapped back up to me.

"Did you sleep with Laura?" Saying the words again made my stomach churn. But I wanted to know...no I *needed* to know.

"Who said that?"

"She did."

Miles chuckled and leaned forward. He dropped his head down for a second before bringing his gaze back up to meet mine. "How could I ever sleep with her?" He moved closer, and my heart felt like it was going to pound out of my chest. "She's not you."

Heat pulsed through my body at his words. My ears rang, and I feared that I'd misheard him. I stared at him, waiting for him to laugh and tell me it was all a joke. That he really loved Laura, and this was a fun prank.

But those words never came. Instead, he grew even more serious as he stared at me. Then, slowly, he slipped his fingers under my chin and tipped my face, so I had no other choice but to look at him.

"She's not you, Shelby. I don't want any other woman but you."

I knew I should speak. I knew I should say something. But words were failing me. This was exactly what I wanted, and yet, I was so stunned that I couldn't react.

And I feared if I didn't say something, and soon, he was going to pull back and I was going to lose him...

Forever.

22

SHELBY

SWEET TEA &
SOUTHERN GENTLEMAN

THE SILENCE between us was palpable. And a second later, Miles dropped his hands and took a step back.

"I want you, Shelby. I've loved you since we were kids. But if that's too much, if you're not ready, I understand."

Tears pricked my eyes. I still had so much wrong with me. I was broken, and he didn't deserve a broken person. Not when I knew I could never be healed. "Miles..." I wiped at my tears, hating that even after everything I was still so weak.

He brought his gaze back up to mine and frowned. He stepped back up to me and brought his thumb to my cheek and wiped. "I don't want you to cry. You've done enough of that. I just want you to let me love you." His fingers lingered on my skin. "I just want to love you."

"But what if I'm too broken, Miles? What if I can never be fixed?"

He stared at me. "We're all a little broken somehow. All we can hope to find in this life is that person who gathers and protects all of our broken pieces until we're ready to heal."

A sob escaped my lips. I'd spent so much of my life fearing what my past had made me become. Fearing that I was never going to be whole again. And yet, Miles didn't see it that way.

He was just waiting for me to be ready to heal.

His hands were on my waist as he pulled me into his chest. I let him hold me as I sobbed into his shirt. There was so much being said between his body and mine, that words weren't necessary.

He shifted so he could slip his arms around my back and my knees and lift me up. I wrapped my arms around his neck and buried my face into his shoulder as he carried me into his room. He laid me on his bed before going to shut the door.

The moon's light shone into the room, lighting the darkness. I curled onto my side and cried into his blankets. Miles dragged over a chair and sat near me, letting me cry like I hadn't for so long.

There was still so much about my past that I needed to face, but the idea that I didn't need to face it alone scared and thrilled me at the same time. My body couldn't seem to process that idea, and the only thing I could do to relieve the stress that had built up inside of me, was to cry.

It didn't help that I was also a little hungover from the shots at the bar.

"Come with me," Miles said, once my tears had subsided and I was just lying there. His hand appeared above me, so I moved onto my back and slipped my hand into his.

He helped me off the bed and guided me over to his bathroom. He turned on the water and took a step back as steam filled the room. He glanced at my dress and then dropped his gaze. "A shower always helps me feel better."

I nodded, chewing on my lip as the heat between us matched the humidity that now coated the mirror and walls. "Okay."

He studied me for a moment, the desire in his gaze so strong that it took my breath away. Then he blinked, breaking our connection, and turned to go.

"Help me?" I asked, desperate to keep him here if only for a few seconds longer.

He paused. "What?"

"With my zipper. Will you help me?" I turned, pulling my hair over my shoulder and exposing my back. When he didn't move right away, I feared that I'd misread the situation until I felt his fingers brush my neck.

Shivers rushed across my skin even though the room felt like it was going to light on fire. I closed my eyes as he gripped the top of my zipper, and the pressure of the dress on my body lessened as he slid it down. His breathing changed as the air around me hit my now exposed skin.

I wondered what he was thinking as he stood there, staring at the lace of my bra and underwear. Did he want me as much as I wanted him?

"There," he murmured, his voice so low that I almost didn't hear him.

I held my dress to my chest as I turned around. "Thanks."

He nodded, his gaze meeting mine. We just stood there as if we were too scared to move. To break the connection that was buzzing between us. I stared at him through my lashes, wanting him to make a move. If he kissed me right now, I would let him.

Suddenly, his hands were on my waist as he pulled me against his body. I let go of my dress which dropped to the floor as I wrapped my arms around his neck. His lips found mine, and my entire body sunk into the feeling of his hands on my bare back, then my waist, then to my shoulder blades.

"Shelby," he whispered for a split second before he crushed his mouth to mine once more.

He lifted me up to meet him, my body pressing against his chest, his hips...everything. I could feel everything. And I wanted to feel more.

I parted my lips and he groaned. Our tongues spun and twirled around each other, tasting, feeling, enjoying. I wanted every part of him, so when he set me down onto the vanity, I wrapped my legs around him, bringing him even closer to me.

He responded by gripping onto my thigh with one hand as his other arm held me firmly around my back. The heat from the shower mixed with the desire we felt for each other had my skin pricking. I wasn't sure where I wanted to go with this. All I knew was that if I didn't stop now, I wasn't going to have the strength to resist. Not when I could feel his fingers drag across my skin and bra strap like he was enjoying the feeling of the lace of my bra.

"Miles," I murmured as I pulled back.

He dropped his head to my neck as he gently pressed kisses across my collarbone. "Shelby," he whispered against my skin.

"I'm not sure I can stop if we go any farther."

He stopped kissing me as my words registered with him. He pulled back and looked at me. "I'm so sorry. Did I take it too far?" He moved to step back, but I shook my head as I wrapped my legs tighter around him, grabbing his shirt to keep him there.

"I want to..." I was scared to meet his gaze, but I forced myself to. "Experience that with you." I chewed my lips, causing his gaze to drift to my mouth. I could see the desire in his gaze. It matched my own.

"But I don't want it to be when I'm half-drunk like this."

He studied me for a moment before he nodded. I unhooked my legs from around his waist, and he helped me down. I fell into his chest, and he just held me against him, his hand holding my head as his cheek was tucked next to me.

"I'll wait for when you're ready," he whispered as he dipped his lips to my ear. The warmth of his breath mixed with the feeling of his mouth next to my skin sent ripples of pleasure through me. "But when you are..." He pulled back and stared at me. "I'll show you exactly how I feel about you."

Desire burned in my stomach, but I knew I needed some more time to heal before I walked into another relationship. Especially a relationship with a man I had so much history with. I needed to be wise for both of us before he and I moved our relationship to that level. Belle was a part of this story, and I needed to think about her as well.

"And I'll do the same," I whispered, chewing my bottom lip as I stared up at him through my hooded eyes.

He quirked an eyebrow and then closed his eyes and tipped his head back. He let out a low moan. "I'm getting out of here before I lose my resolve to stay away from you."

I laughed, but it died down when he walked out of the bathroom and shut the door behind him. Now alone, I hugged myself. This evening had been filled with such extreme emotions that I was left shaking. Partly from desire for the man on the other side of the door and partly because, somewhere inside of me, a dam had broken.

And as much as I wanted to believe that I could heal

quickly, I knew I couldn't. Not when I was as broken as I was.

After I showered, I wrapped a towel around my body and opened the bathroom door. Miles had changed into his pajamas and was lying on his side, propped up by his elbow. He looked up, and as soon as he saw me, he growled and flipped to his back. "Shelby, this isn't fair."

I giggled as I held onto the towel. "I just need something to change into."

He peeked over at me before he jumped off the bed and hurried over to his dresser to pull out a pair of basketball shorts and a t-shirt. He didn't stop when he got close to me, instead, he wrapped his arm around my back and pulled me in for a kiss.

I giggled against his lips, but he didn't let me go. He teased my lips with his tongue until I opened them and let him in. Heat raced through my stomach like hot lava, and I felt myself slipping back into the desire I felt for him.

I wanted him so much. But I was also scared of what that meant for me. So, I pulled back, giving him a scolding look. I pressed my fingers to my lips as a sheepish look passed over his face. He shrugged and then moved to face-plant into the bed.

I changed in the bathroom. When I came back out, Miles was under the covers. He flipped the corner of the comforter over and patted the bed. "I promise, no shenanigans." Then he waggled his finger at me. "I'm not to be taken advantage of."

I laughed and slipped onto the bed, pulling the blankets over my body. He patted his chest and I laid my head down on it, reveling in the sound of his breathing.

He wrapped his arm around my shoulders as his body stilled. "I want you to know that all I've ever wanted to do is protect you. I know we have things to talk about and demons to face, but I want you to know that I will always be here...waiting for you."

I stared at his chest and drew circles with my finger, enjoying the feeling of his soft t-shirt on my fingertips. "I know."

"And when you're ready, I will love you with every part of me." He leaned forward and pressed his lips to the top of my head.

"I know," I said. It was barely a whisper from all the emotions in my throat.

"And when that day comes, I'm going to marry you. Because I never want you to leave." He paused. "I want you to be my wife and Belle's mother."

I closed my eyes as tears filled them once more. It was one thing to feel Miles's love for me. It was something completely different to hear that he wanted me to be Belle's mother. My choices toward Miles and this inn just became that much more real.

I knew I could survive the heartbreak if something happened between me and Miles. After all, I still had a life in New York. I still had Titan, though I hadn't even messaged him since I got here.

But I could never break that little girl's heart. I lived to make her happy. Every choice I made, I needed to keep her in mind.

I was going to do the one thing that the adults in my life never did for me. I was going to think of her.

Not wanting to face the future and what my decisions now meant, I moved to press my lips to Miles's once more and then snuggled against his chest. "Let's talk about it tomorrow," I said as my eyelids grew heavy.

Miles tightened his arm around my shoulders and nodded. "I'll see you in the morning."

Darkness fell around me as my body sunk into the mattress and my mind grew still. I felt safe and protected, and right now, that was all I needed.

The next morning, I woke to an empty bed. I stretched out my hand to feel for Miles, but he was gone. I sat up, feeling disappointed that he wasn't here to wake me up. That he had let me go at some point in the morning.

I pulled off the blankets and slipped my feet onto the floor. After quickly brushing my teeth and fixing my hair so I didn't look like a monster, I padded through the room and out to the hallway. I heard voices as I neared the kitchen, and just as I stepped into the room, Miles stood from the chair he'd been sitting in.

His eyes were wide and his gaze frantic as he started walking over toward me. But then he stopped. "You're up," he said.

I nodded. And the woman he'd been talking to stood

up as well. She was my age, and her eyes were bloodshot as she raked her gaze over me. With a confused look, she focused back on Miles.

"Who is this?" she asked.

Miles glanced between us a few times before his gaze settled on me. He sighed as he extended his hand toward the woman.

"Shelby, meet Tamara." He paused and took in a breath. "This is Belle's mom."

***

I hope you've enjoyed reading The Inn on Harmony Island. There is still so much of Miles and Shelby's story to tell, plus Abigail and new residents on Harmony Island.

Make sure you grab the next book in the Sweet Tea and a Southern Gentleman series, The Shop Around the Corner to find out what happens next!

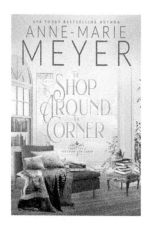

Want more Red Stiletto Bookclub Romances?? Head on over and grab your next read HERE.

For a full reading order of Anne-Marie's books, you can find them HERE.

Or scan below:

Printed in Great Britain
by Amazon

44455784R00169